D0290168

Jenkins
Mighty
Mustang

Sharon Hambrick

Book 2

Illustrated by Mike McDermott

JOURNEY
FORTH™

GREENVILLE, SOUTH CAROLINA

Library of Congress Cataloging-in-Publication Data

Hambrick, Sharon, 1961–
    Arby Jenkins, mighty mustang / Sharon Hambrick.
        p.   cm.
    "Book 2"
    Summary: When he catches Stuart breaking camp rules, eleven-
    year-old Arby decides what to do about this kid who has become his
    nemesis.
    ISBN 0-89084-932-3 (pbk.)
    [1. Camps—Fiction.   2. Christian life—Fiction.]   I. McDermott,
Mike, ill.   II. Title.
PZ7.H1755As   1997
[Fic]—dc21
                                                              97-4984
                                                                CIP
                                                                 AC

Arby Jenkins, Mighty Mustang

Project Editor: Debbie L. Parker

Illustrations by Mike McDermott

©1997 BJU Press
Greenville, South Carolina 29614

ISBN 978-0-89084-932-3

15   14   13   12   11   10   9   8   7   6   5   4

for Brian

*"The just man walketh in
his integrity: his children
are blessed after him."
Proverbs 20:7*

$\mathcal{S}$

Books in the Arby Jenkins series

Contents

1 A Puzzling Situation

I was working on a puzzle when the call came. It was a round jigsaw puzzle that had been constructed, I was sure, by an insane person who wanted to drive me crazy. I pictured this mad puzzle maker singing a tuneless dirge as he thought, *Now how can I confuse and enrage that Jenkins kid?*

It was my own fault that I was going crazy over this puzzle. I had bought it with my own money. Money I should have been saving for camp. I now had a grand total of fifty cents for spending money at camp. This was not enough money to buy a pine cone, let alone a camp shirt or belt buckle. I was a financial disaster, and camp would be here in two short days.

I fingered a border piece and consoled myself. True, I was broke, but at least I wouldn't have to worry about buying a camp hat. My brother Dell had promised to lend me his "official Victory Ranch cowpoke hat" as he called it. He'd bought it last year when he went to camp.

"Let me tell you, little brother," Dell had said to me a few days before, "the fact is I'm going to be making money at the gas station while you're sunburning your nose at camp. You might as well wear the old hat and protect your face."

I was glad enough to borrow the hat. It would save me from having to remember to wear sunscreen, and, more importantly, from having to comb my hair. With a hat, you just put it on. No one sees your hair.

I didn't pay any attention to the telephone ringing because I was engrossed in my own thoughts. Hats. Puzzle pieces. No money. Baseball. My puzzle showed—or would show if I ever finished it—a bunch of jumbled-up baseball cards. I was fingering a piece that looked like it might be half of Babe Ruth's nose when Mom gasped and said, "Oh no!"

I sat bolt upright, listening as hard as I could.

"What do you mean, Chuck?" she asked.

Uncle Chuck is my mom's brother. He and Aunt Margaret live in Cincinnati. Grandma Parsons lives with them.

Something was not right. Was it something about Grandma?

Mom reached out behind her and pulled up a chair. She sat down slowly and nodded her head. "Uh huh," she said. "Okay, I understand."

I stopped pretending to work on the puzzle, put down the Babe Ruth piece, and stared. She said "Uh huh" again, and "Oh no," and "Are you sure?"

Then she said something that scared me. "How long do you think she'll live?"

Grandma Parsons was seventy-eight years old. Pretty old, I thought. Old enough to die.

"Yes, I'm sure that will be just fine," Mom said. I wondered what in the world would be just fine. Grandma dying would not be just fine.

Grandpa Parsons had died when I was in second grade. I was only seven years old at the time, and I missed school for a whole week to go to Cincinnati for the funeral. The car had no air conditioning and no radio. It was cramped, and Dad wouldn't let us take off our seat belts, not even on the open highways where there were no other cars for a hundred miles.

After the service, my family stood in a line at the back of the church. Many people came by to shake our hands and say nice things about Grandpa Parsons. They called him a "pillar of the church" and a "regular Joe." I didn't understand what they meant. Grandpa had always seemed gentle to me, not hard like a pillar. And his name was Howard, not Joe.

I asked my mom later, and she said these were sayings meaning the people liked Grandpa a lot and that he was a good man. I wondered why they didn't just say that.

Most of the people who greeted us were old. Some of the ladies leaned down and kissed me, and I tried to be polite and not wipe the kisses off, but it was hard. I hate to be kissed, unless it's Mom and she's telling me good night.

Grandma Parsons had stood next to my mother as Grandpa's friends filed past. She looked small and breakable, like a porcelain doll. She had white flowers pinned to her black dress, and a hat with a veil. I thought she was beautiful.

Now, it seemed, she would die too.

Mom's voice interrupted my thoughts. "I'll ask John, Chuck. But don't worry. It'll be fine. We've discussed this possibility before, you know. I'll call you back tonight. Maybe I'll see you next week."

Next week? Was Grandma going to die tonight then?

"Yeah, we can stay up all night and play games. That'll be great." She laughed.

What? They're planning to play games before Grandma was even cold in the grave? My mother had turned into a thoughtless, ungrateful daughter right before my eyes.

At last Mom said good-bye and hung up. I looked down at my puzzle as she walked past. To think that she wanted to play games! Maybe Grandma was dead right now. I frowned at my puzzle piece.

Mom must have called Dad from the phone in her bedroom a few minutes later. I was trying to smash a nonborder piece into the puzzle border and wondering why it wouldn't go, when Dad came in the front door and ran straight up the stairs to their room. He was whistling. Whistling!

I snuck upstairs behind him and sat in the hall outside their closed door, under the marks on the wall that show how tall we are.

I could hear my mom's voice, but I couldn't make out the words. Dad spoke more loudly. "It'll be fine, Jane," he said. "Don't worry about it one bit. The kids won't mind at all." His voice sounded firm, not grieved or anguished like it should have been considering that Grandma was dying. And what did he mean *the kids wouldn't mind?*

My sister Staci came out of her room and asked me why I was sitting on the floor in the hall.

"Grandma is dying," I said.

"How do you know?"

"I heard Mom talking to Uncle Chuck on the phone."

"Grandma Parsons?"

"Yes."

Staci, who turned sixteen in June, slid down next to me in the hall and put her legs straight out in front of her. Her long blond hair hung around her shoulders and hid her face. We sat there silently for a few minutes, listening to the sounds of words we could not understand.

"When I was six years old, Grandma taught me how to sew on a button," Staci said. "And I made my first batch of chocolate chip cookies at her house the Christmas I was eight."

She pulled her knees up to her chest, put her arms around them, and cried. Her crying made me cry, and so, when my parents came out of their bedroom, the first thing they saw was two of their three children sitting on the floor crying.

"What's wrong?" Dad asked.

Dad too? Both of my parents seemed heartless, totally unmoved by Grandma's death.

"What do you mean, 'What's wrong?' " Staci said. "Grandma's dying!"

"Oh, honey!" Mom said. She slid down onto the floor and put her arms around Staci. Then she turned to me. "Now, Arby Jenkins," Mom said, "that's what you get for listening to conversations that are not your own."

"Huh?"

"Grandma is not going to die," Dad said firmly. "At least not any time soon."

"What?" said Staci. She looked up at Dad and then over at me. Then she hit me, and I mean she walloped me hard.

"Arby!" she said. "How could you make this up?"

"But I heard Mom say, 'How long will she live?' "

My dad chuckled. "Jane," he said, "we've got to teach this boy not to eavesdrop." He leaned against the wall and laughed.

What is going on? I wondered.

"Get up, everybody," he said. "Let's go downstairs and make some decaf. There are some things we need to talk about as a family." He looked at his watch. "It's almost five. I'll call Dell and tell him to close the station and come home. Then we'll have a good long chat. There are going to be some big changes around here."

I pushed my back against the wall and scrambled to my feet. Then I helped Staci up and stumbled down the stairs after her. She said that she was disgusted with me and that I had made her cry on purpose.

"But Mom said—"

"I don't care." Staci pulled the coffeepot from the coffeemaker and shoved it under the faucet. "Don't say things until you know for sure."

I meekly measured the three-and-a-half scoops of decaffeinated coffee into the filter. Our folks let us drink decaf when we have family conferences. It makes us feel grownup, like we might actually be participating in an adult meeting. I had realized last year, however, that family conferences are times when Dad and Mom tell us what they have already decided.

I got out the sugar and creamer. Coffee really doesn't taste good all by itself.

My dad's gas station is just around the corner, so Dell was home in ten minutes. I was pouring coffee into mugs when he burst into the house and slammed the front door.

Dell is fifteen years old and works at the station for my dad. Now that it was summer, he worked full-time and sometimes, like today, he ran the place when Dad had to be gone. I was kind of glad Dell was gone all day. He had been playing some practical jokes on me lately. Like planting a rubber frog in the shower. That made me scream, let me tell you. Dell was so proud of himself, you'd have thought he'd won the Nobel Prize. At least I had my own room and could have some peace and quiet when I needed it.

Dell was breathing hard as he came into the kitchen at a run. "What's going on?" he said. "Did someone die? Did the house burn down?"

"The house is standing," Dad said. "Look around."

"Oh, yeah." Dell sat down at his regular place. He pulled off his baseball cap and tossed it onto the table. His face and hair were sweaty. He pulled the neck of his T-shirt up over his face and wiped the sweat off.

Staci said, "You're disgusting," just as I placed her steaming mug in front of her. I hoped she was referring to Dell.

"I expected to see fire trucks or something the way you said to come home right away," Dell said. He looked around the table, but no one said anything. "What is so big a deal that the station has to be closed up early on a Saturday afternoon?" he asked.

That's what I wanted to know.

"Grandma's dog Fifi is very ill," Dad said. "Uncle Chuck is going to take Fifi to the vet on Monday to be put to sleep."

Dell coughed and choked on his coffee. He sat back in his chair like he'd been shot. "I had to close up the station because a poodle is going to die?"

A stern look clouded Dad's face.

Dell said "Sorry," and I got the feeling it wasn't Fifi that was the issue here.

"Grandma is very upset about Fifi," Dad said. "Fifi was a great comfort to her after Grandpa died."

Yes, I remembered; she sure was attached to that dog. She took her everywhere. She'd even brought Fifi here on the airplane on her last visit.

"The second thing is this: Aunt Margaret has gotten a job."

"So?" Staci said.

"So, Grandma will have no one to talk with during the day. And with Fifi gone, Grandma will be very lonely."

"So," said Mom, "they think—and we agree—that the best thing for Grandma is for her to move down here with us."

Dell dropped his spoon on the table. I looked down into my coffee. I loved Grandma. But living here? Why did I get the feeling this would change my life?

"The bottom line is," said Dad, "she's coming next week. Mom will go to Cincinnati to pick her up."

Staci asked, "How long will she be here?"

"She is coming to stay. Probably for the rest of her life," Mom said.

Some people live to be a hundred, I thought. She was seventy-eight now. One hundred minus seventy-eight is twenty-two.

"Twenty-two years!" I said out loud. Everyone looked at me. "Never mind," I said. In twenty-two years I would be thirty-three years old. Practically an old person myself.

"Oh, there's one more thing," Dad said. "Grandma will need her own room. You boys are going to have to share."

I didn't bother to say "but, Dad." Dell and I looked at each other in a sort of numb horror and then looked quickly away. I for one did not want to live with a frog hider and belching king. It would be the end of civilized life.

"Share a room with Arby?" Dell said. "I think—"

"I'm sure you think many things, Son. The point is, Grandma needs her own space. You boys will have to share. No, it is not ideal. No, I don't think it will be the best thing that ever happened to you, but it's the way it is. Got it, boys?"

"Yes, sir," we said together. End of discussion. Details later.

Dad laughed. "I knew I could count on you guys. Great." He pushed his chair back from the table and stood up. "I'm going to run back and check on the station."

"Okay if I go with you?" Dell asked.

"Sure."

So Dell and Dad went back to the station, and I went back to my puzzle. I wanted to be fifteen like Dell so I could work at the station and hang out with my dad all summer. I was still only eleven and wouldn't be twelve until August. I fingered a few puzzle pieces. Grandma coming here was fine. Grandma is great. She bakes chocolate chip cookies as good as Mom's and plays a mean game of chess. I have never been able to beat her. Grandma's coming was not a problem. Living with Dell was a problem and not a small one. At least I could ignore it for a couple of weeks while I was at camp. No, probably Dad would want me to skip camp now so I could be home helping get the house ready for Grandma. I'd better face that music right now. Who cared about going to camp anyway?

I trudged up the stairs, walked down the hall past the framed school pictures, and knocked on my mom's door.

"Come in."

She was lying across her bed, leaning on her elbows, with her head propped up in her hands. I sat on the end of the bed and looked at my shoes.

"Mom," I said, "if you want me to skip camp to get ready for Grandma, it's okay. I can stay and help and—"

"Camp!" Mom said. "Oh no!" She became a new person. "Arby, you're not even packed, are you?"

She jumped off the bed and ran down the hall to my room. I followed her, a little bit frightened at the sudden change. Still, I was glad she seemed to be back to her old, energetic self. She flung open the door to my room, uttered a sigh of dismay, and demanded whether I had enough clean clothes to pack.

It is true that there were clothes lying all over the floor. An undeniable mess. Even worse, I'd had a hard time pulling my dirty clothes hamper out of the closet. It was full even without all the dirty clothes that were on the floor. I ran around, shoving more and more clothes into the already loaded hamper while Mom glared at me. It's amazing how many clothes will fit into a hamper.

I was supposed to bring my dirty clothes down to the washing machine when I needed them washed. Obviously, I had fallen behind. Today was Saturday. Mom doesn't do laundry on Sunday, and I was leaving for camp on Monday.

"Get moving, young man." It wasn't her angry "young man," but her military one. It meant I'd better start working, or I would be sorry.

I carried my heavy, overfilled hamper down to the washing machine in the garage. The clothes were packed in so tightly that they wouldn't all dump out when I turned it upside down. I had to pull them out.

Mom came down a couple of minutes later and helped me sort the clothes. She thought I had two or three full loads to do.

"Mom," I said, "could we build a room for Grandma or something?" We piled blue jeans into the washer. I measured the detergent.

"Maybe later," she said. "Can't do it in a weekend."

Of course I knew that.

"I could live in a tent in the back yard," I said.

Mom came over and hugged me. I hugged her back and was glad the garage door was closed and nobody was around.

"I know what you're thinking, Arb," she said. "Believe me, I know. I had to share a room with my little sister my whole life. Oh my! Come on, Arb. Let's have ice cream."

We went inside and had ice cream. It was going to be dinner time in about an hour, but it didn't seem to matter. Mom dipped her spoon into her chocolate swirl and held it up before her face. "Sometimes emotional discussions require the smooth, creamy comfort of ice cream. Take it from me."

I believed her.

She told me about the days when she and her sister Lisa shared a room. "The worst part was dividing the cleaning—who would clean what. We stooped to all sorts of scheming, threatenings, promises—anything to get out of cleaning." Mom laughed and stirred her ice cream.

I like to stir my ice cream too, so that it gets all soft and mushy. "But Aunt Lisa isn't disgusting like Dell is."

"Girls can be disgusting too." She smiled.

I didn't believe it.

"It'll be okay. And, by the way—"

"Yes, Mom?"

"Really, I understand. Lots of kids have to share rooms all the time. Sometimes with more than one brother. But you know, we'll see what we can do. Maybe later, we can build on. If Grandma likes it here and decides she wants to stay always, she has some money for things like that."

I sighed. What a relief.

"But there will be at least several months of sharing a room. You'll be fine." She scraped the last bit of ice cream from the sides of the dish. "You know, I think I'll be having this conversation later with Dell. I'd better save room for more ice cream."

I cleared the dishes and set the table for dinner. It hadn't occurred to me at all that Dell might think it would be disgusting to live with *me*.

2 Had a Little Dog

The bus bumped over the potholed road, and I couldn't help wondering why I had eaten three chili dogs for lunch. I had looked forward to camp for several months, but now with the chili dogs and a large order of onion rings jostling for position in my stomach, I couldn't keep my mind on camp.

My best friend, Ray Sanchez, was sitting next to me. He and the other guys on the bus were singing a song about fleas on a dog. This song goes higher and higher in pitch with every verse, so that by the end of the song everyone is singing in a high soprano that would make your ears hurt on the best of days. And let me tell you, this was not one of my better days.

It was Dell's fault. He had insisted that we celebrate my first trip to camp by eating lunch at Big Pete's Famous Burgers, a place my dad calls a greasy spoon. My mom says Big Pete's is a disgrace to health-conscious America, but she did order an extra large plate of French fries and a bacon cheeseburger to go with her diet soda.

Halfway through my onion rings, I realized that Dell was not celebrating the fact that I was able to go to camp at last; he was happy that I'd be gone for two weeks. This occurred to me right before he asked me if he could have a few onion rings.

"No way," I said. "You can have all the onion rings you want for two weeks while I'm at camp eating s'mores."

S'mores are made by smashing a roasted marshmallow between two pieces of a chocolate candy bar. This combination is placed between two halves of a graham cracker. It's a gooey, melty, delicious sandwich.

Once when our family was camping, we'd made s'mores. My first marshmallow caught fire, so it was black and crunchy, but the chocolate made up for it. Mom let me make four s'mores that night. I couldn't believe it. Mom is usually very careful about what we eat.

"I figured since we were saving money by camping instead of staying in a motel, we could at least indulge in chocolate," Mom had said. All us kids agreed and said "Way to go, Mom," but Dad gave her a funny look.

Anyway, the four s'mores were delicious, but I didn't sleep well that night. When I groaned and said I had a stomachache, Dad showed no mercy.

"He who eats four s'mores," he said, "shall suffer the consequences."

At camp, I was sure, they'd only let us have one s'more.

Thinking of s'mores didn't help matters in my interior. As the bus negotiated the winding road, the chili dogs slammed against the onion rings, and the whole business was sloshed around with Dr. Pepper.

I knew better than to look at the millions of pine trees flipping past. If your insides are doing gymnastics, you should look at something steady, something that is not moving. So, to distract myself, I stared at the baseball hat of the kid in front of me. A tag hung out the back of the hat that said "Great American Hats. Made in China."

The kid's name was Stuart Baltz. I had met him in the parking lot as we were handing our suitcases and sleeping bags up to Coach Smithers. Coach was the bus driver, and he was tying our stuff onto the luggage rack when Stuart walked up.

Ray had introduced us.

"Arby," he had said, "this is Stuart Baltz, Mrs. Stinson's grandson. He's living with her now."

"Hi, Stu," I said.

"Stuart," he replied. "Not Stu, Stuart."

"Hi, Stuart," I said.

"Hi, Four-Eyes."

I cringed. "Just call me Arby." It hadn't been my idea to wear my glasses to camp. I had contacts, but Mom said there was absolutely no way she was going to let me take them to camp.

"Look, Arb," she had said, "if you lose your glasses, or break them at camp, you'll still have your contacts for school. If you lose your contacts at camp, it'll be glasses all school year for you. Is this what you want?"

No, I did not want that. I might not be the smartest kid in the Western Hemisphere, but I knew enough to know I'd rather wear contacts than glasses to junior high school.

Stuart's four-eyes comment had hit me hard, and only by great effort was I able to overcome my desire to punch him in the nose.

"Have you lived with Mrs. Stinson long?" I asked.

"Oh, yeah, Grandma Ellie's great. We've been there about a month."

"Oh," I said. "You haven't been at Sunday school, have you? I don't remember—"

"Sunday school? Not a chance. I don't do that Bible stuff."

Oh. I didn't know how to reply to that. I'd never met anyone before who didn't do "Bible stuff."

I changed the subject. "Is it nice at Mrs. Stinson's? I like how she plays the organ."

Mrs. Stinson played the organ once a month for special music at the evening service. She always played the same song: "Like a River Glorious." I know all the verses because every time Mrs. Stinson plays this song, my mom sings it all the way home.

"Yeah, it's nice. Grandma Ellie's rich. She gave me fifty dollars for spending money at camp! How much spending money do you have?"

"Fifty—" I said, shocked. Fifty dollars. The kid had fifty dollars!

"You've got fifty dollars too?" Stuart asked.

"No."

"So, how much do you have, then?"

"Fifty cents." I dug my toe into the ground.

"Fifty cents! Ha ha. Whoa. I guess you'll be buying up stuff like it's going out of style." Stuart had slapped me on the back. "You should have asked your grandma like I did. She just whipped out her purse and handed me fifty big ones. I'm telling you, she's the best."

As the bus bounced along the road, I stared at Stuart's "Made in China" hat, feeling like I was going to explode, while Ray and the other guys were still singing that awful flea song. Ray himself was singing really high, like a bad soprano in a low-budget opera. I jabbed him with my elbow.

"Be quiet, will you, Ray? I'm in agony."

Ray looked over at me. "Arb! You're green!"

He scrambled up onto his knees and turned to the boy behind us. "Hey, Doug, help me get the window down. Arby's sick!"

I sat hunched over while Ray and Doug clambered over me to get the window down. Don't ask me why, but bus windows never work easily. They always take two people and they only come down halfway, so of course, even when the window was down, I didn't get the effects of the fresh air.

Ray sized up the situation immediately. "Hey everybody!" he said. "Arby's sick. Put the windows down."

The boys obeyed with a kind of frantic hurry. They must have been afraid of what might happen if I was allowed to feel bad too long. A cool swoosh of fresh air filled the bus, and boy, was I glad. I breathed in lungfuls of good clean mountain air. *Whew.*

That's when I heard the deep voice of the bus driver, Coach Smithers. He was singing very low, like the bottom notes of the piano. I could barely make out the words. More people joined in. Now I could understand them clearly. I groaned.

Ray cheered "Right on, Coach!" and started to sing that dreadful song again:

Had a little dog, skinny as a rail.

He had fleas all over his tail.

Every time his tail went flop

The fleas on the bottom all hopped on top.

The song went on and on, getting higher and higher with each repetition. I had two thoughts. One was "I'm so glad I can breathe again," and the other was "Don't they know any other song?"

3 Vicissitudes of Life

At last we drove beneath a rough wooden arch painted with the words *Victory Ranch*. The bus ground to a stop on the gravel parking lot.

"Okay, boys! Out you go."

A rush of boys tumbled out of the bus and onto good hard ground. Coach Smithers climbed the ladder to the luggage rack and crouched on top of the bus, untying ropes. We waited impatiently below. Other buses arrived. Cars pulled in, and boys jumped out of them, dragging suitcases and sleeping bags.

At last Coach flung aside the ropes and tossed the sleeping bags down. They landed with dull thuds on the ground, scattering little clouds of dust. As each boy picked up his bag, he brushed off a smudge of dirt.

My sleeping bag was dark blue. It landed squarely in front of me.

"Good aim, Coach!"

"Only the best for my boys," he said.

After the sleeping bags were down, we formed a sort of bucket brigade at the back of the bus. A couple of guys got onto the ladder. Coach handed a suitcase to the top boy, who handed it down to the next boy, who handed it down to me. I put the suitcases on the ground in a line. Finally, the ladder boys and Coach came down from the bus. Coach looped a long piece of rope around his hand and elbow like my mom does with yarn. He tossed the rope through the open door of the bus, then turned to face us.

"Well, boys," Coach said, "this is it."

A vague, disturbing feeling crept into my heart. How was I going to survive this place? I had never been here before. I didn't know what to do. I—

"Let's go, Arb," Ray said.

My heart relaxed. Ray's here. Of course everything will be fine. Best friends and camp—nothing could be better.

We made a straggly line and walked toward a large sign that said "Check-In This Way."

Everywhere I looked, boys about my age were emerging from cars and buses. Little brothers hung onto them. Mothers hovered. Sisters pretended not to be jealous that this was Boys Only week at Victory Ranch.

Staci used to go to camp during Girls Only week, but this summer she was working with Dell at my dad's gas station. The subject of Staci's working at the station had caused a scene at the dinner table one night because Dell couldn't get it through his head that a girl could pump gas.

"Look, Dell," Staci had said, "Mom pumps her own gas all the time. Pass the mustard, please."

"That's different," Dell said. He passed her the mustard. "She's not getting paid for it."

"But well she might be," Dad said, and this ended the discussion. So Staci works four days a week. She smiles at the customers and makes good tips.

I swung my sleeping bag around in a full circle, pretending nothing was bothering me. Pretending I wasn't a million miles from home. At least Ray was here.

"Hey, Ray," I said, "you brought your signaler, didn't you?"

"Of course. I can't even consider using a regular flashlight anymore," Ray said.

A few months ago, Ray had found a couple of old signal flashlights in his basement. They were like ordinary flashlights, but a little button on the switch can be pushed to make the light go on and off. Ray and I learned Morse code from charts in the encyclopedia. All spring we had signaled each other from our rooftops at night.

I'd brought my signaler to camp too. You never know when a signaler will come in handy.

The Check-In sign directed us into a large open room that was filled with people. Ray explained that this was the dining hall. Boys stood in the long check-in line while mothers stood by their suitcases. Little brothers and sisters ran around. A couple of babies cried, and one mother had a baby in each arm.

I nudged Ray. "Hey, Ray, maybe it will be quieter here than at home, huh?"

"You know it," he said. Ray has twin baby sisters. They are a year old, and they cry a lot. "Maybe I'll get some sleep."

We moved a few feet forward. I thought we'd never get to the front of the line. I counted thirty-five boys ahead of us.

"Did you pack your toothbrush, honey?" a woman said in a loud voice. The whole room could have heard her. How awful to have your mother ask "Did you pack your toothbrush?" in front of a million people.

"When we get to the front of this line we'll find out which wagon we're in," Ray said.

At Victory Ranch, campers sleep in covered wagons. There are six bunks in each cabin—five for campers and one for the counselor—and the wagons have western names. Ray had told me all this last year. He'd lived in a wagon called "Old Paint."

I had wanted to go to camp last year too, but we couldn't afford it. Ray had filled me in on all the details of camp though, so now I couldn't wait for the campfires, the hikes, the canoeing, and the s'mores.

At the front of the line a man sat behind a table. He wore a cowboy hat and a string tie. As we got closer, I could read his name tag—Cowboy Phil. Ray had told me about him too. Last year he'd stood up in a canoe and capsized it. A whole boatload of kids had gotten drenched, and Cowboy Phil had lost his hat. The hat he wore now looked new.

Finally it was our turn. Ray was in front of me.

"Name?" Cowboy Phil asked.

"Ray Sanchez."

"Been here before?"

"Yes, sir. Last year."

Cowboy Phil looked through a card file for a few seconds and then pulled out a card with Ray's name on it.

"Okay, Sanchez. You're in Appaloosa Junction. It's the third wagon from the left in the wagon train."

Ray said, "Thank you," and stepped aside to wait for me.

"Name?"

"Arby Jenkins."

"Been here before?"

"No, sir. This is my first time."

He flipped through the cards again and pulled out my card.

"Jenkins, you're in Mustang Hollow. It's the first wagon on the right in the wagon train."

What did he mean I was in Mustang Hollow?

"There must be some mistake," I said. "I should be in Appaloosa Junction with Ray."

"Ray who?" asked Cowboy Phil.

"Ray Sanchez, my friend right here. He's in Appaloosa Junction."

"He is, but you're not. It's Mustang Hollow for you, pardner. Next!"

I stood stock-still, not moving, until the kid behind me nudged me out of the way with his sleeping bag. I stumbled off, forcing myself to put one foot in front of the other. I could vaguely hear Cowboy Phil saying "Name? Been here before?" as I followed Ray out of the dining hall.

I couldn't believe I was not in Appaloosa Junction with him. Mustang Hollow. Whoever heard of Mustang Hollow anyway?

"Don't worry, Arb," said Ray. "You'll be fine. There will be four other guys in there. Maybe one of them will be from our church. It'll be great. Come on!"

Ray was eager to get going. "Yeah," I said, "it'll be great."

I followed him past a long low building that had a lot of windows in it. There were signs on the doors. One of the signs said "Trail Boss." Ray told me the Trail Boss was the camp director. Through the window we saw him talking on the telephone. He was leaning back in his chair and his feet were propped on his desk. The window was open and we could hear every word he said.

"No, ma'am," the Trail Boss said. "Unless it's an emergency, the campers are not allowed to call home. Your son will be fine. Don't worry about a thing, ma'am. We'll take good care of him."

Too bad, I thought. I wanted to call my mom right now. If Mom were here she would make sure I was in Appaloosa Junction where I belonged.

I had asked her to drive Ray and me to camp, but she said no doubt the social benefits of riding the bus outweighed the creature comforts of riding in an air-conditioned car with music piped through quadraphonic speakers. What she meant was "Why should I drive you when the bus is going anyway?"

Ray's voice broke in on my thoughts. "Why would anyone want to call his mother during camp?" he asked.

"Maybe if a kid was homesick he might want to call," I said. My suitcase was heavy, and it banged against my leg.

"Homesick?" Ray said, swinging his sleeping bag around in a full circle. "Who could be homesick at Victory Ranch?"

I didn't say anything. How could I admit to being homesick after spending a grand total of twenty-five minutes at camp? I would be in seventh grade in a few weeks. Junior highers shouldn't get homesick.

The door beyond the Trail Boss's had a sign that said "Doc's Hideaway."

"That's the nurse's office," Ray said.

"Why is it called Doc's if it belongs to the nurse?" I asked.

"Maybe because Nurse's Hideaway doesn't sound very cowboyish."

As we walked past the door, it opened. A man with a cowboy hat on his head and a stethoscope around his neck leaned against the door frame. His name tag said *Cowboy Brian, RN*.

"Howdy pardners," he said. "Gotta check your heartbeat. You can't be a camper if you don't have a heartbeat."

"Okay," said Ray. "You can check."

Cowboy Brian put the stethoscope on Ray's chest and listened. "Yep, it's beating. You can go ahead."

"Thanks, Doc," said Ray.

"That's *nurse*—Cowboy Brian, registered nurse," said Cowboy Brian. "Best medical care this side of the Mississippi. You get sick from overeating yourself, be sure to come see me. Break your leg on a hike—they'll bring you right here."

"It's weird," I said to Ray as we walked toward the wagon train. "Staci's a gas station attendant, and the nurse is a man."

"These are the vicissitudes of life, Arb," said Ray.

"Huh? What's a vicissitude?"

"Search me," Ray said. "It's just what my dad always says when I don't understand something. I think it means he doesn't understand it either, but that's the way it is."

Sort of like being in a different covered wagon than Ray. I don't get it, but there it is. Vicissitudes indeed.

4 Four-Eyes

Ray left me at the entrance to the wagon train, a circle of brightly colored covered wagons surrounded by huge pine trees. He bounded away to Appaloosa Junction while I turned and walked slowly to Mustang Hollow.

The wagon itself was bright red, with the words *Mustang Hollow* painted in gold on the side. The canvas cover was beige. I hoped it wouldn't leak if there was any rain.

A tall man leaned against the side of the wagon. He was carving a piece of wood with his big, rough hands. Gray hair showed beneath his cowboy hat. Gray hair! He was probably as old as my dad, which was forty, and which was not what I had expected. Counselors, I thought, were supposed to be young. Ray's counselor last year was a college student named Tiger who could burp the whole alphabet without taking a breath.

"Let me guess," said the tall man. "You're Mike, Arby, or Dan." He looked at my sleeping bag. My initials "AJ" were written in fat letters on the outside.

"Arby, right?" said the tall man.

"Right," I said.

"I'm Cowboy Joe," he said. "I'll be your counselor for the next two weeks. Let's go inside and get you settled."

Cowboy Joe took my sleeping bag and walked up the ladder and into the wagon. I followed, dragging my heavy suitcase. I wished I hadn't had to bring so many clothes.

"You only need two pairs of jeans," Dell had said. "One to wear and one in reserve in case you fall in the mud or someone pushes you into the lake."

Staci had said, "That's disgusting! Two pairs of jeans for two whole weeks," but I had smiled at Dell. It's a guy thing. Why change clothes if you don't have to?

However, Mom's word was law, so I'd packed six full changes of clothes. Used carefully, she said, these would last me through camp. Dell had punched me in the arm. "Two pairs, Arb. Trust me." Now I wished I could have followed his advice.

The inside of the covered wagon was small. It was taken up with a set of bunks, three high, on each side. There was a narrow walking space between the bunks. A boy was unrolling his sleeping bag in the middle bunk on the left side. Another boy sat cross-legged on the top right bunk. It was that Stuart kid. He was not on my top-ten list of people I wanted to live with for two weeks.

Stuart sat like a bag of flour on his bunk, no expression on his face. He didn't speak or move. Weird kid, I thought. He was still wearing his Chinese-American baseball hat.

Cowboy Joe got right to introductions.

"Arby Jenkins, this is Drew Peters," he said, pointing to the boy on the left middle bunk.

"Glad to meet you," I said.

"Hi," said Drew. He smiled.

"And this is Stuart Baltz," said Cowboy Joe.

"We met on the bus," I said.

"Oh, yeah," Stuart said. "It's my friend Four-Eyes."

I turned red and felt the urge to climb up to his bunk and punch him.

Cowboy Joe spoke sternly. "Stuart, we are not going to have any kind of speech like that in this wagon or anywhere in the camp. Is that clear?"

"Hey," said Stuart, "can I help it if the kid's got dumb glasses?"

"Apologize," said Cowboy Joe.

"And he gets sick on buses." Stuart laughed and slapped his baseball hat on his leg. "The whole bus had to jump to attention because Four-Eyes here was going to lose his lunch."

"Apologize." Cowboy Joe took a step toward Stuart's bunk. I wondered if he believed in spanking.

"Okay, fine. Sorry, Arby," said Stuart.

It was not the most sincere apology I had ever received, but I said, "That's okay," when it was definitely not okay.

This was not the way to start camp. Camp was supposed to be fun. Camp was not supposed to start with losing my friend to Appaloosa Junction, being banished to Mustang Hollow, and being cooped up with a mean kid who called me names.

I shoved my things onto the bunk directly underneath Stuart's. I'd chosen that bunk so I wouldn't have to see Stuart when I was lying in bed. I unrolled my sleeping bag and slid my suitcase to the end of the bunk where there was an open space past the end of the mattress.

Why do I have to be in the same wagon with this creepy kid? I wondered. Probably it's more of those vicissitudes.

5 Real Work

After a few minutes, Mike and Dan showed up. Mike took the top bunk across from Stuart, and Dan took the bottom bunk under me. Cowboy Joe had claimed the other bottom bunk. There were books and papers scattered over his sleeping bag, and he had an alarm clock that ticked loudly.

"Well, boys," said Cowboy Joe as soon as everyone had been introduced and the sleeping bags were unrolled. "Welcome to Mustang Hollow."

He stood in the narrow walkway and smiled. I smiled back. He seemed like a nice enough man, and honestly, I get to hear enough burping at home.

Cowboy Joe announced that we were going to be the best wagon in the whole camp and that we were, in fact, the Mighty Mustangs of Mustang Hollow. I didn't feel very mighty, especially after the four-eyes comment. Cowboy Joe didn't seem very mighty either, but at least he was nice.

"In what way are we mighty?" Stuart asked.

I groaned out loud, picked up my pillow, and smashed it into my face. I hate it when kids ask questions like that. Why couldn't he just sit there like the rest of us, and wait to hear what the counselor was going to say next? Who cared why we were or were not mighty? Cowboy Joe probably said this to get us bonded together. Sort of like when Coach makes us do cheers for ourselves before a game. It seems conceited, but it makes us play harder.

Cowboy Joe must have never heard such a question before because he thought for a long time before he spoke. Maybe he too was thinking we were not mighty at all. Or maybe he was getting sick and tired of Stuart's bad attitude. I knew I was. Two weeks seemed like a terribly long time to sleep on the bunk beneath a kid who called me names and had the nerve to ask the counselor in what way we Mustang Hollowers were mighty.

"We are mighty," Cowboy Joe said at last, "because I say so."

I had strategically placed myself so that I couldn't see Stuart, and I didn't know how he reacted, but the other guys said, "Yeah." I had a feeling that Stuart was still sitting there like mold on cheese.

"And furthermore," said Cowboy Joe, "I intend for the Mighty Mustangs of the glorious Mustang Hollow to be the greatest bunch of cowpokes this camp has ever seen!"

His voice had been rising as he made this speech, and we all clapped and cheered. Except Stuart, of course. I could tell he wasn't participating because Drew, who was sitting across from me, looked up at Stuart, then looked at me and rolled his eyes. I smiled at Drew and laughed aloud.

After the pep talk, Cowboy Joe took us on a grand tour of the camp. We saw the swimming pool and the showers, the craft shop and the dining hall.

"I hate camp food," said Stuart.

"Shut up, Stuart," Dan said. "For your information, nobody cares what you think about the food."

Whoa. That shut Stuart up pretty good, and right now. My dad never lets me say "shut up," but I was glad someone had said it. We weren't allowed to say "stupid" either.

The next stop on the tour was the campfire circle. We sat in the first row of seats.

"This," said Cowboy Joe, "is where the real work of camp happens."

"What work?" asked Mike.

"The work of the heart," said Cowboy Joe. "Every night, after the day's activities are over, we will come here to sing and to listen to the Trail Boss tell us about the Lord. I'm praying the Lord will work in all our hearts."

Stuart groaned.

"The Lord?" he said. "Do you mean God? Do you mean I have to come down here every night and listen to some old guy talk about God? I thought camp was supposed to be fun."

"Stuart," said Cowboy Joe looking straight at him, "I'm sorry you don't know Jesus as your Savior. I'm sorry you don't understand about the love of God. I hope you'll come to know Him while you're here at camp."

"Know God?" Stuart groaned again. "You guys sound like my grandma. It's all she ever talks about when she's not playing that creaky organ of hers. I thought I could get away from that stuff by coming up to camp. Guess I was wrong, huh?"

"Yes, Stuart. You were wrong." Cowboy Joe spoke softly. "Victory Ranch is a Christian camp, and it's my job as your counselor to keep you safe, well-fed, and learning about God. There's work to be done in everyone's heart. In my heart, in all the guys' hearts, and in your heart, Stuart. You'll see."

"Nobody's messing with my heart," Stuart said. "My heart is just fine, thank you very much."

6 Spaghetti Friends

Cowboy Joe took us up to the Activities Sign-Up next. We were allowed to choose two activities to learn during the first week of camp.

I scanned the list of choices: archery, canoeing, hiking, leather craft, horseback riding (costs extra), swimming, guitar, woodworking.

Horseback riding was out. My parents would never agree to the extra expense. They had already paid a lot of money for camp.

Way back in January I had promised them that I would help with camp expenses, but somehow there was always something I wanted to buy whenever I had any money. Once during the spring I had $2.17. But then I batted a baseball through my neighbor's window. Bingo! Instant bankruptcy.

I considered the list of activities thoughtfully. I wanted to be with Ray. Camp would be funner if I had a couple of chances to talk with Ray. Also, I did not want to be in any classes with Stuart. He bothered me, and though I didn't want to admit it, I was afraid of him. I'd never met anyone in my life who said flat out they didn't care about the Bible and didn't want to know God.

"Stuart," I said, "what activities are you going to sign up for?"

"Who wants to know?"

"I want to know." I didn't look at him.

"Why?"

I should have seen that question from a mile away. What could I say? I couldn't very well tell him that I wanted to know what classes he was taking so that I could sign up for something else. If I replied to Stuart, "Well, Stuart, frankly you make me sick and I want to be as far away from you as possible," my dad would hear me, drive up to camp, and deliver a stern lecture or a swift spanking.

"Just asking," I said. I turned to look at the leather watchbands on the counter by the leather craft sign-up sheet. I saw Ray's signature on this sheet, so I added mine at the bottom. Stuart walked up beside me and picked up the watchband. It had horses imprinted down the middle and little leaves along the edge.

"I don't have a watch," Stuart said. "But my grandma will get me one if I ask her. She's got bags of money."

"I thought you had fifty dollars," I said. "Buy your own watch."

"That's all you know," he said. "Not everyone has had money his whole life. Maybe I want to save up for something."

I looked up at him in surprise. He was intently staring at the watchband and fingering the horse imprints.

"It'd sure be nice to have a watchband," said Stuart, more softly now, "in case Grandma someday buys me a watch."

I didn't get it. Stuart had fifty dollars—or so he said. Watches are cheap—once I got one free for buying a children's meal at Big Pete's. So why couldn't Stuart just buy a watch?

My heart sank as he signed up for leather craft. There went one class.

I walked quickly away, saw Ray's name on the canoeing list, and wrote my name in my best cursive handwriting. Then immediately I wished I had written it sloppily, unrecognizably, so Stuart wouldn't be able to read it. Stuart, in spite of his rudeness, seemed to think maybe I'd be his friend. So perhaps he was going to sign up for all the classes I was in, just like I wanted to sign up for the classes Ray was in. I suddenly wanted to be as far away from the canoeing sign-up list as I could get.

I left the room to wait for Cowboy Joe and the rest of the guys. I looked at the pine trees, hundreds of them standing there like all was right with the world. And the blue sky . . . it just hung up there as if nothing was wrong. And the squirrels. Hopping around, unaware that an innocent kid named Arby was trapped in a wagon with a pathetic excuse for a twelve-year-old.

I wondered when I would be allowed to run around and have fun. I wondered if I was ever going to see Ray again, or if he was imprisoned in Appaloosa Junction with the Mighty Appaloosas. I wondered whether needing general advice from Mom and Dad qualified as a big enough emergency to get around the no-telephone rule. I wondered whether Dell was right when he said that the first dinner at camp is always boiled slugs and worm salad.

Dinner was salad without worms and spaghetti that looked like worms but wasn't. If it had been worms, I wouldn't have noticed because I loaded on the Parmesan cheese so thickly I really couldn't taste the spaghetti. It's like my dad says, "Spaghetti is the medium for the cheese." I'm not sure exactly what that means, other than go ahead and sprinkle on a lot of cheese and enjoy it. Mom disagrees; she says that I'd like the spaghetti without cheese if I'd give it a chance.

We had garlic bread with our spaghetti. The camp cook didn't make it exactly right. Mom puts Parmesan cheese on the garlic bread before baking it. This makes the world's best bread, but maybe they didn't know that at Victory Ranch.

I sat across the table from Drew, and we talked between mouthfuls. It turned out he was from a church on the other side of our town and that he went to Hope School.

"You go to Hope?" This was astonishing news. Hope School was my school's rival, and I hadn't thought any normal people went there. "I thought all you guys had fangs."

"Oh, you must go to Greenhaven," he said.

I nodded.

"Don't worry," he said, lowering his voice like we were forming a conspiracy. "We won't tell anyone we're friends when we're back at school."

"Greenhaven?" It was Stuart's voice. "Do you mean Greenhaven Christian Academy?"

"Yes," I said.

Stuart slammed his fork down onto the table. "For crying out loud, that's the dumb school I have to go to this year," he said. "It figures a dorky kid like you would be there."

"So don't go," I said. "It's a free country."

"Not for me it isn't." He planted his elbows on the table. "My grandma's making me go. She told my mom we could live with her if I promised that I'd go to school at dumb old Greenhaven."

I hoped desperately that Drew wouldn't laugh and say, "Yeah, right, dumb old Greenhaven," like I might have said if the conversation was about Hope School.

"Greenhaven's a good school," Drew said. "I don't think anybody bites. Hey, Arb, nobody bites, do they?"

"No one bites."

Stuart made a sound of disgust and plunged his fork into his spaghetti.

I was disgusted too. Not only did I have to live with this obnoxious kid for two entire weeks but he was also coming to infect my school with his bad attitude and mean comments. He'd probably end up being my locker partner. He'd probably have an assigned seat next to mine in every single class.

In my frustration I twirled an enormous amount of spaghetti onto my fork and crammed it into my mouth. It was way too much and I knew it. I had barely enough jaw movement to chew. I could feel spaghetti sauce oozing out the corners of my mouth just as Drew spoke.

"Did you play Spring Ball for Greenhaven, Arby?" Drew asked.

I wanted to cry. Here was the perfect moment for making an incredible impression, an unforgettable statement about winning the last game. But I couldn't speak until I had finished off that wretched mouthful of spaghetti.

This was not the way to impress a boy from Hope School who had just defended the honor of Greenhaven. It took me a full minute to get down this one bite of food, and I followed it with a long drink of ice water.

Then I sat up straight and tried to sound triumphant. "Yes, I was on that team. I hit the double that won our team the last game."

Surely this statement would cause Drew to see what a great baseball player I was.

"Hey, I remember. Right over my head. Oh well, I won't hold it against you, Arby," he said. "We can be friends anyway. Hey, look—chocolate cake!"

So much for being impressed. Still, he'd said *friends.* Maybe camp wouldn't be such a disaster after all. He'd also said *chocolate cake.* That rang my bell. I looked down the table and saw the cake tray. Chocolate cake with chocolate frosting. Without a doubt, my favorite kind.

Cowboy Joe took a piece and passed the tray to Drew.

"One piece, guys," he said.

When the tray got to Stuart, he took a piece, then another.

"One piece, Stuart." Cowboy Joe's voice was stern, unbending.

"Oh, sorry," Stuart said, "I'll put it back." He placed the second piece of chocolate cake back on the tray.

Then, as he was about to pass the tray to Mike, he exploded with an obviously fake sneeze. "Aaa-chooo!" He sneezed all over the cake tray, spitting on all the cake.

"Stuart!" Cowboy Joe rose from the bench, grabbed Stuart by the arm, and yanked him from the dining hall.

What a lousy kid, that Stuart. It was like he went out of his way to irritate and disgust people he wanted to be friends with. Well, it was working.

Stuart had wrecked my cake, spoiled everyone's meal, called me names, and to top it all off he had signed up for leather craft, and would no doubt want to sit by me in every class. Didn't he have enough brains to know that wrecking people's lives is not the way to make friends?

"What are we going to do, guys?" asked Drew. He cut his piece of cake in half and handed me one of the halves.

"Let's get up a petition and get him sent home," Mike said. "Stuart is a loser. The sooner he's gone the better."

"Yeah," said Dan, "or maybe we could muzzle him. Shutting him up would be an improvement for sure. I never saw such a bad attitude."

I nodded. What were we going to do about it?

"That's not what I meant," said Drew. "What I mean is—well, look, guys, Stuart's not saved. He needs to be saved. What are we going to do about it? How can we show him that he needs to be saved?"

I swallowed hard, which wasn't easy because of the lump in my throat. Drew was one hundred percent correct, and I hadn't seen it or wanted to see it. I had just wanted to figure out a way to get away from Stuart.

I scraped the frosting from my half-piece of cake and licked it off my fork. I felt about three inches tall and about as gushy inside as the boiled slug Dell had threatened would be dinner. Couldn't camp just be fun? Did it have to be complicated by having to show God's love to a bad kid?

I guessed maybe Cowboy Joe was right—there was work to be done in my heart after all.

7 The Mighty Mustangs

"It's songfest, cowpokes," Cowboy Phil said. We had finished eating, and the tables were being cleared. "We'll start with some easy ones."

Cowboy Phil played the guitar and led the singing. He started with some silly songs. I didn't know them. Then we did some I-Love-Camp songs about rolling hills and daffodils. I knew a couple of those. It felt good to sing after such a jam-packed emotional day. Surely now things would relax. No doubt Cowboy Joe had flattened Stuart's illusions and brought him back to planet Earth.

During songfest, Cowboy Joe led Stuart back into the dining hall. They sat down together at the end of the table. Both of them looked solemn. Aha, I thought. Cowboy Joe sure gave him the time of day.

I felt sorry for Cowboy Joe. It must be awful for him to have such a rotten kid in his wagon.

"I can see we've got some newcomers to Victory Ranch," Cowboy Phil said. "The singing's kind of weak. Let's do one everyone knows. Raise your hand if you know 'I've Been Working on the Railroad.' "

Everyone knew this song. Even Stuart joined in.

He must be made of iron, I thought. If I had been hauled out of the dining hall in disgrace like he had been, I would have crawled back in like a worm after the rain. No way would I be singing "Dinah won't you blow your horn?" Probably he was used to getting into major trouble.

After songfest, the Trail Boss made the announcements. "There will be free time after dinner until seven o'clock."

Yes! Free time at last. I could run around. I could breathe. I could get away from Stuart and maybe see Ray! A smattering of applause greeted this announcement. I guessed I wasn't the only one who needed a breather.

"At seven o'clock," he continued, "all campers will meet at the wagon train for the famous First Night Roundup!"

All the boys who had been at camp before whistled and stomped their feet.

Joining the uproar seemed like the thing to do. I stomped and clapped even though I had not one clue what the First Night Roundup was. From where I sat, I could see the Appaloosa Junction table. Ray was waving his hands in the air and hollering "Whoo-whoo" and grinning from ear to ear.

Hey, wait a minute, I thought. How can he have so much fun when I'm not even in his wagon? Then I looked across the table at Drew and saw him clapping his hands over his head. What was all the hullabaloo?

"And now," shouted the Trail Boss above the din, "to discuss the particulars of the Roundup, I am proud to present our resident Rounder-Upper, the incredible medical Cowboy Brian!"

All previous shouting was nothing compared to the deafening roar as Cowboy Brian, RN, walked to the front of the dining room. He waved and grinned at us like he was the grand marshal of the Rose Parade.

As if they had been pulled by strings, boys all over the dining hall jumped to their feet and chanted "Cowboy Brian, Cowboy Brian!" No way did I want to be left out of this scene. I jumped up and shouted too. It was loud. If noise could shake a building, we would have shivered the dining hall to splinters.

"Okey-dokey, cow-pokeys!" Cowboy Brian shouted into the microphone. "It's Roundup time at Victory Ranch!"

The tumult never let up. It was clear from the look on Cowboy Brian's face that he enjoyed this moment immensely.

He's a nurse, I thought. I've never known a shouting nurse before. A nurse shouting into a microphone at a hundred boys.

What would Dad think, I wondered, if I came home from camp and announced I wanted to become a nurse? I knew perfectly well what Dell would say. Dell gives out opinions free of charge on any subject. He would lean back against the nearest wall, shove his hands into his jeans pockets, and blow my ego to shreds.

"A nurse?" he'd say. "What a sissy you've turned out to be." Mom would defend my choice and talk about the great need for Christian nurses all over the world. She would make Dell apologize. He would say "Sorry," and I would still feel like a sissy.

At last the din diminished.

"Tonight's Roundup game will be team duck-duck-goose!" Cowboy Brian said.

A low rumble grew around me. Everyone was muttering the same things: "Huh?"

"Team duck-duck-goose?"

"What in the world is that?"

"OKAY!" Cowboy Brian shouted in capitals. It scared me and I jumped. "Don't worry that you've never heard of this before. It's easy. I should know because I made it up! Here are the rules. Listen carefully because when the game starts at exactly seven o'clock, you will have to know what to do!"

The last time I had played duck-duck-goose was in first grade. Back then we sat in circles, waited until someone tapped us on the shoulder, and then got up and tried to catch them. It was a recess game, a little kid game.

Team duck-duck-goose as described by Cowboy Brian, on the other hand, would be a serious contest of speed and endurance.

"Remember! Each wagon is its own team, so play hard for your wagon, and may the best cowpokes win!"

Cowboy Brian sauntered back to his table amid thunderous applause. He sat down, picked up half a piece of cake on his fork, and gulped it down. No chocolate frosting smears on his face. No crumbs on his chin. Cowboy Brian was smooth, cool, and important.

Suddenly, I wanted to be a nurse—specifically, a camp nurse. Dell could say what he liked.

The wagons were arranged in a circle, and at seven o'clock sharp, every camper was sitting Indian-style in front of his wagon. The counselors then arranged us so that each wagon group was evenly spaced around the circle. I ended up between James from Pinto Valley and Terrence from Appaloosa Junction. I told Terrence that my best friend Ray was in Appaloosa Junction.

"Sanchez? He's cool."

Sanchez. I never called Ray by his last name. Dell calls all his friends by their last names. Maybe it's something he picked up at camp.

A whistle blew. I jumped up into a sort of crouch, tensed and ready to run. Drew had given us a big speech back at the wagon, and the Mighty Mustangs were ready to win.

"Okay, guys," Drew had said, "it's time we pull together as a team! Let's get out there and show everyone who's the best wagon!"

"Yea!" we had shouted, and even Stuart smiled. Perhaps things were going to come together at last. Whatever Cowboy Joe had said to Stuart must have done some good. Cowboy Joe came up the ladder into the wagon just as we were shouting.

"So," Cowboy Joe said, "does this mean the Mighty Mustangs are poised and ready to win?"

"Yes, sir!" we said.

When the whistle blew, Cowboy Brian touched someone on the far side of the circle to be *It*. *It* walked slowly, and he shouted loudly so we could all hear. "Duck!" He touched a boy on the head. He continued walking and saying "Duck" as he tapped several people on the head. Then at last he shouted "Goose!" as he tapped a boy on the head.

The Goose was Stuart, and the instant he was tapped, all the Mighty Mustangs took off running. At the same moment, the boys from *It*'s team started to run too. The object was for the Goose's team—us, in this case—to catch as many of *It*'s team as we could before they got back around to their places.

I shifted into turbo power and caught the boy I was chasing. He shouted, "Ah, bummer!" but I kept running, trying to catch the other guys on his team.

The whole camp was screaming and shouting for one team or the other. By the time I got back to my place, I was winded. But I had tagged my man and I was happy. Stuart had caught *It* without any trouble. He had also caught another one of the guys on *It*'s team. Stuart could run like a scared cheetah, and I was glad, for once, that he was on my team.

For the next round, Stuart was *It.* So when he tagged a person to be the Goose, we tore around the circle again. I was a little slower this time, and I got tagged. Stuart didn't get tagged. He was "the wind on the loose" for speed.

The rounds went fast, and there were many, many rounds. Everyone got a chance to run several times. Everyone was panting and sweating. The Mighty Mustangs made a great team effort, and thanks to Stuart's lightning speed, I figured we had done pretty well in points.

When the whistle blew to signal the end of the game, I was huffing and puffing, and my legs were shaky. The Trail Boss walked to the center of the wagon train.

"Okay, campers! What a game! Let's hear it for us all!"

We raised a worn-out, exhausted cheer.

"I'm happy to announce the winners of tonight's Roundup!" More cheering. My stomach twisted into tight knots. Sweat poured down my face.

"Third place goes to Morgan Manor!"

The boys from Morgan Manor jumped to their feet and shouted, "Morgan! Morgan!"

"Second place goes to Colt Corner!"

A Colt boy ran into the center of the circle and turned three cartwheels.

"And first place goes to the Mighty Mustangs of Mustang Hollow!"

I jumped up and punched the air with my fist and ran to the middle of the circle with the other Mustangs. We pounded each other on the back. Drew threw his head back like a coyote and howled.

Cowboy Joe walked with casual stride to the center and made a low bow to the assembled camp. We were the Mighty Mustangs at last!

Now, if only Stuart would be as nice as he was athletic, everything would be perfect.

8 Not My Call

The campfire burned with tall, snapping flames as the Mighty Mustangs filed into the last row of benches. It was cold, and I wrapped my heavy coat tightly around me. Cowboy Phil played the guitar. It was hymn time now, so I knew these songs. It reminded me of home when Mom played the piano and we all gathered around her to sing.

The Appaloosas sat next to us, so Ray and I got in snatches of conversation between songs.

"How's it going, Arby? Isn't camp great?" he asked.

"Yeah, especially since we won the Roundup!"

"That was great," he said.

I grabbed Ray's arm. "Look!" I leaned close to Ray and whispered. "See that kid sneaking off over there?" I pointed behind us and through the trees.

"That's Stuart," I said. "Can you believe he would actually ditch campfire?"

I nudged Ray and nodded again to Stuart's retreating form. "Should I say anything, Ray? Look, he's going off toward the wagons!"

"Calm down, Arb. He probably just forgot his Bible," Ray said. He picked up a pine cone and pulled one of the seeds out. He held it high and then dropped it. It spun like a helicopter rotor as it fell.

"Maybe," I said. But I didn't mean it.

I slid behind the other guys and whispered to Cowboy Joe. "I saw Stuart walking away, Cowboy Joe. He's leaving."

"It's okay," said Cowboy Joe. "I said he could. He forgot his Bible. He'll be right back."

Talk about feeling like a tattletale. I slunk back to my place. I sat hunched up and humiliated through all four verses of "Amazing Grace."

I nudged Ray again.

"What?"

"Why couldn't he just share someone else's Bible?" I didn't buy the line about the forgotten Bible one bit. Stuart was cutting out on campfire, plain and simple. I had a sudden urge to go after him, to find out what he was doing.

"Arby, let it go. It's not your call," Ray said. He dropped another spinner.

Not your call. That's what Coach Smithers always said when we didn't agree with the umpire at a game. If something is not your call, then don't worry about it. This is a nice way of saying "It's none of your business" and "Let the ump do his job." Or in this case, the counselor.

I sighed and began to focus on the fire. The dancing flames were multi-colored—yellow, orange, red—mixed up and flickering into the night. When I paint fire in a picture, I make the flames orange. It's funny how I never noticed all the colors before.

After song time, the Trail Boss gave a talk about the stars. He told us that when we look up into the night sky, although it seems like the stars are just tossed up any which way, each one was actually placed there by God. He read us a verse that said God knows each star by name. He also said that the longer a person studies the stars, the more interesting they become.

"So you see, boys," he said, "the millions and millions of stars tossed up against the blackness of space are known individually by God. He created them and knows them.

"More importantly, God knows each of you personally. He sees what you do, and He knows your thoughts, even the motivations behind your actions. In fact, He loves you, and though you are a sinner, He made a way to save you—by sending His Son, Jesus Christ, to pay for your sins."

I looked down the row. There was Stuart, Bible on his lap, sitting right next to Cowboy Joe. Perhaps I had misjudged him after all. I wondered if the Trail Boss's words had made any impression on him. Apparently not. He was looking at the ground, not even paying attention. And the message was almost over. Probably he hadn't heard a word of it.

"Just as God orders the paths of the solar system and all the stars, so too He has ordered your life," the Trail Boss said. "Is your life filled with trials? God has ordered it. He can see you through. Trust Him."

Life ordered by God. Now that was a big thought. Grandma coming to live with us. Me stuck in a wagon with Stuart at camp and in a room with Dell at home. Why had God ordered these things for me?

The Trail Boss encouraged each of us to examine our hearts to see if we were trusting the Lord Jesus for our salvation. He told us to see a counselor if we needed spiritual help. Then Cowboy Phil strummed one of my Dad's favorite songs: "Take My Life and Let It Be."

This song used to bother me because the first part says "Take my life" and the very next phrase is "Let it be." That didn't make any sense to me, so I got up my nerve and asked my Sunday school teacher one Sunday. He showed me how it's important to look at the whole sentence when finding a meaning. The whole phrase is "let it be consecrated, Lord, to

Thee." The problem is taking a breath at the wrong time and wrecking the end of the sentence.

I thought hymns must be sort of like the stars. Sort of like dancing flames. Maybe even sort of like Stuart. Until you take the time to study them, figure them out, they might not make a whole lot of sense. The thing was, though, I didn't want to take the time to figure out Stuart. I wanted him to get his act together without any help from me whatsoever.

I was engrossed in my own thoughts, so when Ray pushed me, I jumped.

"I said good-bye, Arby. Wake up! Earth to Arby."

"Oh, sorry. I was thinking," I said.

"So I noticed. Well, have a good night."

"Thanks, Ray. See you tomorrow in leather craft."

"Yeah," Ray said. "That will be great."

I walked at the tail end of the Mustang line on the way back to our wagon. Stuart was scuffing his feet along the dirt at the back of the pack with me.

"Jenkins," he said, "do you really believe this God stuff?"

"Yes," I said.

"I mean really, about Jesus being God's Son and all that stuff?"

"Yes." I thought I had turned into a kettledrum the way my heart pounded in my chest.

"Well, I don't." He made a mighty kick at a mound of dirt and sent it flying in every direction. "I don't believe a word of it."

9 What?

I didn't sleep well that night. Stuart's words whirled around in my brain. *"I don't believe a word of it."*

There was no getting around it. Stuart was not a Christian and didn't want to be a Christian. Well, that was that, then, right?

But Drew's words pounded in my head also. *"What are we going to do?"*

What indeed? What could a bunch of eleven- and twelve-year-olds do to get a kid like Stuart to see he needed Jesus? I was not a happy camper. Camp was supposed to be a fun couple of weeks of hiking, swimming, canoeing, and eating dessert every single night. Camp was not supposed to keep me up late wondering what I could do about the salvation of a kid who didn't want to know God.

I wanted to call my dad. I tried to think what Dad would say, what my pastor would say. But I couldn't. All I could see were the dancing flames. All I could hear were Stuart's words, *"I don't believe a word of it."*

10 Modern Art

I was the scraper at breakfast on Tuesday morning. At meals there are two jobs. The hopper goes to the kitchen to ask for anything that's needed at the table, such as more ice water or more rice or a rag to clean up spilled milk. Drew was the hopper Tuesday morning. He had to get a rag because he told a joke that made Dan laugh so hard that milk came out of his nose.

"I shall gladly go get the rag," said Drew, "but I refuse to swab the deck."

The other job at meals is scraping, and since I was the scraper this morning, I sat at the end of the table. After everyone finished eating, all the plates were passed down to me, and I scraped all the leftovers onto one plate. The result was an oozy, sloppy mess that my sister would have called gross and disgusting, but which I thought was extremely cool.

The best part was when the syrup oozed into the scrambled eggs. This combination reminded me of one of the pictures in the modern art section of our local art gallery.

I was deep in thought, wondering whether I could paint a picture of this plateful of wasted food and sell it for a million dollars. So I didn't hear most of the activities director's announcement about morning classes. All I heard was: ". . . those people will go to archery instead of leather craft."

"What people?" I said to Mike, suddenly alarmed.

"The people who were last on the sign-up list," he said.

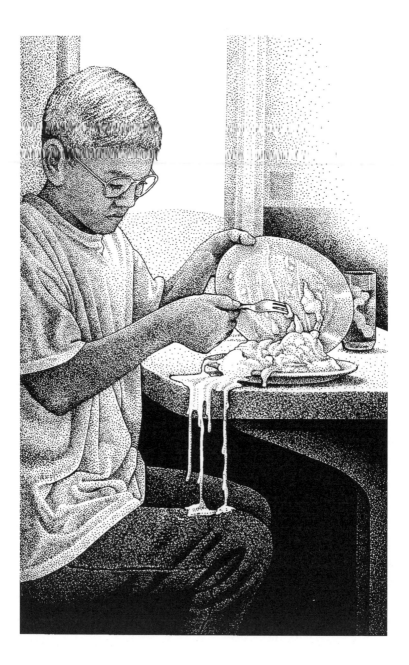

"How do I know if I'm still in the leather-craft class?" I asked, frantically scraping plates. I wanted to be in leather craft. Ray was in leather craft. Besides, archery was a thing I did not want to do.

In archery, you have to hold your bow exactly right, fit the arrow perfectly, aim with precision, and then let fly the arrow with great force and incredible accuracy. Then, if you're even a millimeter off one way or the other, you don't get a bull's eye. This kind of exactness was beyond me. I had tried, believe me.

When I was eight years old, I tried archery at the Greenhaven City Park on the Fourth of July. I missed, and we're not talking about millimeters. I missed the entire target by several feet. People said, "Good try," and I managed to slink away.

"Ask at the craft shop after breakfast," Mike said. Then, as if to comfort me, he added, "Don't sweat it, Arby. Archery's fun."

Fun for him, maybe.

A pile of scrambled eggs fell with a sickening plop onto my mountain of scraped food. Syrup dripped over the edge of the too-full plate and onto my jeans.

In consequence of this, my jeans stuck to my leg, making it difficult to carry the plates back to the kitchen. Still, walking back and forth from the table to the kitchen wasn't so bad. It released some of the pent-up nervous energy I had from thinking about archery and the fact that Stuart would probably be in archery too.

It was true that Stuart ran like an Olympic champion. I had to admit he had won the Roundup for us last night. That didn't make up for the fact that he was rude and that he flat out did not believe the Bible and that he complained about everything. Even the night before, when we were all exhausted, he had been nothing but a nuisance.

"How can anyone be expected to sleep on these boards?" he had asked last night.

"Go to sleep, Stuart," said Cowboy Joe. "It's been a long day."

"Right," said Stuart. "Sleep on a board in a smelly old borrowed sleeping bag in a wagon with a bunch of guys who snore."

This is what Mrs. Peterson would call a prepositional-phrase overload, and more words than I wanted to hear from Stuart for the rest of my life.

"Stuart," I'd said, "why is your sleeping bag borrowed?"

"Because, dummy," he replied, "I don't have one."

I was determined not to let his "dummy" comment stop me. "Why don't you have one? Doesn't your family go camping?"

There was silence for a long time. I thought he had fallen asleep at last.

"No. We don't go camping."

I tried again. "I thought your grandma was rich and would buy you anything," I said, but Stuart hadn't answered.

Anyway, after breakfast, sticky jeans and all, I ran to the craft shop. Sure enough, too many guys had signed up for leather craft, so Stuart and I had been switched to archery.

As I stood there trying to figure out how to get out of archery and away from Stuart, Stuart himself walked into the room and leaned against the counter.

"Is archery the only option?" he asked. "I hate archery."

"Nope," said the activities director. "There's still room in the horseback riding class. Always is. Costs extra to ride. Want to try that?"

I watched Stuart's face as closely as I could without being too obvious. I didn't want him to think I cared what class he took. I considered the situation. If I took horseback riding and Stuart stuck with archery, I wouldn't have him hanging around me all the time. My folks wouldn't know about the extra cost until they got the bill after camp. I could tell them that all the other classes had been full.

"Well, son," the activities director said to Stuart, "what'll it be? Horseback riding?"

"Nah," said Stuart. "I don't ride."

Here was my ticket to freedom. I could promise Mom and Dad that I would pay them back the extra money. Horseback riding would be perfect. No archery. No Stuart.

"I'll do archery," Stuart said.

Decision time. All I had to do to be rid of Stuart—at least for this one class—was to sign up for horseback riding and worry about the expense later.

I loved riding. When I was little, we used to go to the pony rides at the county fair every year. And when we visited my Aunt Donna in Montana, she packed a picnic lunch, and we rode her horses out to the fishpond Uncle Jim had dug with a backhoe.

Now, here at last, another possible happy horse experience was within reach. All I had to do was tell one teeny little lie. I could even confess later and apologize. I would promise to pay my parents back double, triple even.

It didn't work. My conscience wouldn't fall for it.

"Put me down for archery." I managed a twisted sort of smile, shoved my hands in my pockets, and trudged out the door. Stuart was right behind me. Figures.

11 Robin Hood Meets His Match

"All right, guys," said Cowboy Eddy. "Welcome to the archery field."

Cowboy Eddy was the counselor for the boys in Old Paint and also our archery teacher. He scanned the row of boys facing him on the archery field. I am sure we looked pretty pathetic. Stuart stood by me, and he looked pathetic.

"Do I look as pathetic as I feel?" I asked him.

"Worse," he said.

"Have you ever shot arrows before?" Stuart asked me. He sounded nervous. I wondered if he wished, like I did, that he had signed up for horseback riding.

"Once," I replied. "It was a disaster. I didn't even hit the target. What about you?"

"Never," said Stuart. "We never do anything."

"Oh."

The good thing was that surely Cowboy Eddy wouldn't be expecting expert bowmanship out of us. Most kids, no doubt, don't practice archery on a regular basis. One kid, however, seemed to think he was a twenty-first century Robin Hood. He swaggered through us boys acting like this was Sherwood Forest and we were his band of merry men. He was a big kid—maybe an eighth grader—and he talked loudly.

"Bull's-eye city," he said. "Just keep your eyes on me, kids. I'll show you how it's done."

Cowboy Eddy had obviously met this type of boy before. "Back in line, buddy," he said, nudging Robin back into the group of boys.

Cowboy Eddy showed us how to stand, how to hold our bows, and how to fit the arrow on the string.

Four targets stood twenty five yards away. That was seventy-five feet, which seemed like an awfully long way for those fifth graders, or even for me, to shoot an arrow. Come to think of it, twenty-five *feet* would have been out of my range.

The fifth graders got to shoot first. Robin Hood walked up to one of them and offered to help him just as the boy was pulling back the string. I edged closer to hear what he said. Stuart tagged close beside me.

"Let me help you," Robin Hood said to the boy.

"That's entirely unnecessary," said the boy. He had on those horrible black glasses that my father wore as a kid and I make fun of, and he spoke as if the phrase "entirely unnecessary" was part of his usual vocabulary.

Stuart snickered and elbow-jabbed me in the ribs. I grinned. There was going to be fireworks here, I just knew it. We took a few steps closer.

"Don't be silly," said Robin. "Now, let me help you."

"I assure you I do not need your help. Please step back."

"Fine," said Robin loudly. Then he faced everyone and said to no one in particular. "The kid doesn't need my help. Fine. Just fine."

The fifth grader let the arrow fly. It landed smack in the middle of the target, and the whole class burst into cheers.

Stuart really let loose. "Fine!" he shouted. "Just fine!"

I looked over at Robin Hood. He had turned a deep shade of purple and had shoved his hands into his pockets. There was no place for him to hide.

"Bull's eye!" shouted Cowboy Eddy, running up to the best archery shot at Victory Ranch. "What's your name, son?"

"Jared. Jared Spence."

"That's good shooting, Jared. I can't hit the bull's eye myself very often," said Cowboy Eddy.

"Lucky shot," said Robin Hood.

"Not at all," said Jared, looking straight into Robin's face. "I get a lot of practice." He let that thought sink in before adding, "My dad owns an archery shop."

I laughed out loud. What a relief to realize that no matter how badly I did in archery, I wasn't going to be the most humiliated person in camp that day.

I didn't do so bad. At least I hit the target a couple of times, which is way better than that day at the park. Of course, I have glasses now, which helps a lot. Back in those days I couldn't see anything, so perhaps that had added to my shooting inability.

Stuart did well, too, especially considering it was his first time. He almost made a bull's eye on his third shot. I think the wind blew his arrow a little bit because it sure looked like a straight shot to me.

Stuart was a natural athlete, I decided. The way he had run the night before and the way he was zinging out arrows like he'd been shooting all his life impressed me greatly. I'm good at academic stuff like spelling and writing compositions, but I stand in awe of anyone who's a born sportsman.

At the end of class, I volunteered to help Cowboy Eddy pack up the bows and arrows and return them to the storage shed. Stuart volunteered too. I wished Stuart wouldn't hang around me so much, but I figured it was going to happen for the rest of camp and I had better get used to it. I couldn't bear to think what it would be like at school next year. What if Stuart wanted to hang around me all through seventh grade?

"How long have you been teaching archery?" I asked Cowboy Eddy. We were out on the archery range collecting arrows.

"This is my first year," he said. "I sell insurance when I'm not a cowboy."

"You mean like car insurance?" Stuart asked. "My mom says car insurance is way too expensive."

"Yep," Cowboy Eddy said. "And life insurance and home owners insurance and boat insurance."

"Boat insurance?" Stuart and I said together.

"Yep," he said. "If you bought a boat, and it capsized and sank, you would want to get some insurance money for it."

"If I got a boat," I said, "it would never capsize."

"Yeah," said Stuart.

It was funny to think that Cowboy Eddy sold insurance. I guess I thought counselors just lived at camp all the time. Like teachers. I never thought that teachers had homes to go to, but every once in a while, I'd see my teacher, Mrs. Peterson, at the grocery store and wonder what she was doing there.

"What about you?" Cowboy Eddy asked me. "Ever done any archery before?"

"No, sir," I answered. "I'm a board game man myself."

"Board games!" he said. "Now there's a sport for you."

I couldn't tell if he was kidding or not, and I was a little embarrassed. I didn't want him to think we just sat around and played ordinary games by the ordinary rules.

"Of course," I said, "at my house we never play by the rules more than once."

"What?" said Stuart. "You don't play by the rules? I thought you were a goody-goody Christian, always doing what people told you."

"Games are just for fun," I said. "They don't involve authority."

"Good point," said Cowboy Eddy. "Sometimes it's fun to modify a game. Like when you get money for landing on Free Parking in Monopoly."

"Oh, yeah," said Stuart. "That's the best. Mom and I play Monopoly like that. One time I had all the five hundreds and we had to cut up paper for the bank to have some." He laughed.

"Chess," I said, "is the only game that cannot be modified." I knew this because Dell and I had tried various ways of modifying it, but they didn't work very well. If you let the castles move diagonally or let the pawns attack head-on, it gets confusing.

"Ah ha!" said Cowboy Eddy. "This just proves that you've never tried horse chess."

"Horse chess?" asked Stuart and I together.

"Yes, horse chess," said Cowboy Eddy. "An invention and modification of my own." He paused, and in the silence I realized I was up against a master game-modifier.

"In horse chess, the queen can move as a knight."

This thought stunned me. A queen can already move in any direction she wants for as many open spaces as she wants. But for her to be able to move as a knight—two up, one over or one up and two over—would put a whole new twist on the game.

I had an intense urge to run to my wagon and scribble off a note to Dell, asking him to try this game with Staci and let me know how it went. I love chess. As soon as Grandma got here—

The thought of Grandma coming hit me again. Every so often, even though I was far away from home, the thought of Grandma Parsons coming and Dell moving in with me ran over me like an out-of-control bus.

I sighed. I'd probably never get to try horse chess, let alone become any good at it. I could see it clearly. There I'd be, sitting in my room, playing horse chess with Staci. Suddenly, Dell and his buddies would burst into the room, belching nursery rhymes and startling me into knocking over my king. Staci would jump up saying "oh gross" and "oh, you're so disgusting," and run out of the room.

"Hey, Arby, come on." Stuart's shouting got my attention back to the real world, and I grabbed my pile of bows and ran to the storage shed

12 Have S'more

Tuesday night at dinner, Cowboy Joe told us not to eat any dessert.

"No dessert?" asked Drew.

"None," said Cowboy Joe.

"Why?" we five said together.

"I have my reasons," he replied. "Trust me."

So the hopper did not go to the kitchen to get the dessert, and our whole table looked around enviously as the rest of the boys enjoyed their dessert, which was apple cobbler with vanilla ice cream.

"This had better be good," said Stuart, and for once I agreed with him.

After dinner, we went back to the wagon. Cowboy Joe said we didn't have to brush our teeth just yet. We grinned and slapped each other high-fives. When a grownup says after dinner that you don't have to brush your teeth just yet, it means more food is coming. Cowboy Joe told us to take our flashlights in case we weren't back before dark and to carry a coat, in case it got too cold. It wasn't cold yet, but it does get cold during the night at camp because of the higher elevation. I had argued with my mom about bringing a coat, but I was glad I'd given in at last. She was right. As always. It got plenty cold here.

Cowboy Joe led us on a walk down a narrow path between the trees. I joined in as we sang the fleas-on-the-dog song.

The song did not improve through my singing. We Mighty Mustangs made jokes and sang out loudly at the tops of our lungs as we hiked down the dirt trail.

"Cowboy Eddy sells insurance in his regular job," I said to everyone in general.

"Hey, Cowboy Joe," said Mike, "what's your regular job?"

"I'm a high school principal."

"No way!" we said, stopping still in our tracks. Principals are supposed to be scary. You're not really supposed to like them, and you're certainly not supposed to have one for a camp counselor.

Cowboy Joe laughed. "Don't just stand there, guys. Let's get going."

We got going and I mean right now. When a principal tells you to get going, well then, you don't stand there doing nothing.

"What school, Cowboy Joe?" asked Drew.

"Hey, should we call you Mr. Cowboy Joe?" asked Dan.

"It's a special school. I work with kids who've been in trouble with the law," Cowboy Joe replied. "And no 'mister,' please. Cowboy Joe is fine. I come up here to get away from being a principal."

It never occurred to me that a principal would want to be de-principaled for a while. Made sense, though. Especially for a principal of a reform school. So, things weren't always pine cones and squirrels for Cowboy Joe either. He probably spent his days breaking up fights, talking to rough kids, and working with police officers.

Stuart's behavior is nothing compared to some of the guys Cowboy Joe's worked with, I thought. This comforted me. I now knew Stuart would never be too much for Cowboy Joe. Better yet, Stuart knew it too.

We walked a long way to a clearing; it had a fire ring. Under Cowboy Joe's direction, we ran around gathering small sticks and bits of wood for kindling. We arranged the kindling at the base of what was going to be our fire. Then we got some bigger pieces and finally a couple of good-sized logs. I wondered if Cowboy Joe was going to make us rub sticks together to light the fire, but he had a small box of matches, and I breathed a little easier.

"Notice that there's a large clearing here," he said. "Never build a fire too close to trees, especially when it's summer. The wood is dryer and can ignite easily."

When the fire was going pretty well, Cowboy Joe went with us into the trees and instructed us how to find a nice green stick on a tree. We each found one, and we got an extra one for Drew, who was tending the fire. Cowboy Joe cut them off for us with his pocketknife. These, he told us, were our skewers.

Naturally, we were sword fighting in the clearing within seconds.

"En garde," shouted Mike.

"Ya!" I shouted, leaping to face him and brandishing my sword.

"Okay, guys. You can sword fight, or you can have s'mores," said Cowboy Joe. "Which is it?"

Instantly the sword fight ended. We crowded around Cowboy Joe, the best high school principal in the whole world, while he handed out marshmallows for us to roast.

The thing to know about s'mores is this: they are messy. Even the regular way, and Cowboy Joe was not going to let us make them the regular way.

"Peanut butter," he said. "Peanut butter s'mores are the best thing going this side of the border."

What border he was referring to, I did not know, nor did I care. A peanut butter s'more was the thing I now realized I had been missing out on through eleven and a half long, wasted years.

I slathered peanut butter onto my two graham crackers, then broke a chocolate bar in half and stuck one half onto each gooey cracker. Then I roasted my marshmallow. Carefully I slid the almost-burned marshmallow off my stick and in between the chocolate bars. The concoction melted together and ran down my arm, but I didn't care.

The first bite was the best thing I had ever tasted. Within seconds the whole thing was gone. I sat staring into the starlit sky, savoring the moment. I wished I had eaten my s'more more slowly.

"Who's ready for another?" Cowboy Joe asked.

"Yea!" There was a rush on Cowboy Joe and his sack of provisions.

Cowboy Joe seemed to have an unlimited supply of chocolate bars, which amazed me, because I can only get one on special occasions at home or when I spend my own money.

My dad once told me that when he was a kid, chocolate bars cost twenty-five cents. I told him that those days were gone forever, and he made me a speech about the value of a dollar and inflation, the Federal Reserve, and the money supply.

None of this made any sense to me, but Cowboy Joe's supply of chocolate made sense, and I suddenly wanted to be a principal in a reform school when I grew up, if that was where he made enough money to buy all the chocolate in the world.

I slathered peanut butter and roasted marshmallows and ate six superdeluxe s'mores. I should have known better, of course. I should have remembered the last time I had s'mores. I had only eaten four that time—and those without peanut butter—and I'd had an uncomfortable night. Now here I was, miles from home and far from Cowboy Brian's nurse's station, downing superdeluxes as if they were popcorn.

13 My Discovery

We made it back to camp in time for campfire. I really wished we hadn't because bed is what I chiefly needed at that moment. I needed to be horizontal, prone, stretched-out, and sleeping. No one should ever be allowed to eat six super-deluxe s'mores in one sitting.

As we walked back to camp, however, and everyone around me was skipping and jumping around and kicking pine cones, it occurred to me that I was the only one whose insides were knocking him out. Perhaps in my excitement over the unlimited chocolate resources, I had overdone it by eating six when everyone else only had two or three.

"How many did you have?" I asked Drew. I pretended to be fine. I smiled and laughed with everyone else. I could not let on that I had stuffed myself past decency.

"Seven!" Drew said. There was triumph in his voice.

Seven, I thought. Now that boy is a master. Seven s'mores, and he's trooping along as if nothing's happened.

"I have never had so much chocolate in my life," said Stuart. "Never in all my life." He said this with finality, as if there was nothing more to be said.

I began at this moment—in spite of my flip-flopping insides—to consider all the unanswered questions I had about Stuart. Why did he live with his grandma and why had she sent him to camp? Why was it that his family had never been camping? Why did he not own a sleeping bag? Did they not have much money? Did they not like the outdoors? How often did he play Monopoly with his mom? Did he ever get to eat chocolate?

Stuart's comment about the chocolate got right down to where I lived. I realized that things were going on in his life that I knew nothing about. I wondered if Stuart, like the stars the Trail Boss had talked about, would get more understandable the more I got to know about him.

As we sat down around the campfire that night, I decided that come what may, I was going to find out about this kid. I was going to dig deep and find a way to get to know him. Maybe I could even help him be saved. It wouldn't be easy, that was for sure. But I would try.

This resolve made me feel better in my spirit, but it did nothing at all for my fragile physical condition. I deteriorated throughout the singing, and by the time Cowboy Phil switched from the peppy songs to the slow hymns, I was wretched. I put my head down between my knees.

Cowboy Joe came up behind me and tapped me on the shoulder. "You all right, Jenkins?" he whispered.

"I ate six s'mores, Cowboy Joe," I said. "Can I go lie down?"

"Do you need to see the nurse?" he asked.

"No, I'll be okay if I can stretch out on my bed."

"Okay, go ahead," he said. "Be careful. Use your flashlight."

I crept away as quickly as I could. I didn't want to disturb anyone at the campfire, and I didn't want anyone to know I had been conquered and laid out flat by a couple of burned-up marshmallows and a few Hershey bars.

It was dark, so I turned on my flashlight. Tripping over a rock and falling on my face would not be a good thing right now.

In order to get to the wagon train, I had to walk by the long low building where the camp offices are. I was concentrating on going carefully and quietly, so when I heard a voice coming from the Trail Boss's office, I gasped. It was Stuart's voice, I was certain. He had snuck away from campfire again, and now I knew why.

"It's all right, Mom," he said. "Oh yeah, they let kids call home all the time. Don't worry about it. How's your job going?"

I switched my flashlight off and backed against the building. The door to the Trail Boss's office was closed, but the window was open and I could hear every word Stuart said. I knew I needed to get past the window without him seeing me, so I crouched down and crawled as quietly as I could under the window to the other side. I was pretty sure that he wouldn't talk long. Whatever excuse he'd given Cowboy Joe—if he'd said anything—he couldn't miss an entire campfire service. I was certain he'd only talk a few minutes and then sneak back to the campfire as if he had never left.

"Please, Mom," he said, "can you come and get me? This place is like church all day long. It's the worst."

He listened for a while, and said "uh huh" a few times.

"Oh, the counselor's okay. He gave us lots of chocolate tonight." He was silent again, and I wondered what his mom was saying on the other end of the line.

"I could help out, you know, if I were home."

Stuart's voice was sad when he said that. I wondered why his mom needed help. Was Mrs. Stinson ill? Was the talk about her having a lot of money a lie? Did Stuart need to go home and get a paper route to make money? And why, I finally thought, does he never mention his dad? Doesn't Stuart have a father at all?

Maybe his dad had moved away. I knew several people whose fathers had left home. It scared me to think about what life at my house would be like if my dad weren't around.

"Please, Mom," he was begging now. "All they talk about here is God. I want to come home. The guys are okay, except that they're a bunch of Christians, just like Grandma. They make me feel rotten. That's why I want to come home."

I thought hard. Had we guys ever made fun of Stuart or called him a sinner? Had we done anything to make him feel bad? I couldn't think of anything. Could it be that Stuart was feeling bad about his sin because of what he heard at campfire time?

After a few minutes I realized that I needed to get to my wagon right away so I could lie down. I crept away as quietly as I could, but with my flashlight turned off I didn't see the big stick lying in my path. I stepped straight on it. It broke with a loud crack.

"I gotta go, Mom," Stuart said quickly. "Other kids are waiting to use the phone."

I heard him say "I love you" just as I got past the building and out of sight.

I struggled up the ladder and into my bunk.

It must have been several hours later when I awoke with a start from a nightmare. I sat up straight in bed, sweating and breathing hard. Everyone else was asleep. Cowboy Joe was snoring, and I could hear the tick-tock of his alarm clock. I got out of bed as quietly as I could, taking my flashlight with me. The dream had scared me, and I wanted to get out of the wagon and get some fresh air.

I sat on the bottom rung of our ladder and shone my flashlight between my feet, so as not to disturb anyone else. I had dreamed that Stuart and I had both gotten sick and had been locked up together in Doc's Hideaway. In my dream Stuart kept saying "we're stuck forever. Forever, forever," in a high, screaming voice.

I sat on the step for a long time, calming myself with the knowledge that I wouldn't be stuck anywhere forever because I was saved. I would go to heaven when I died, and if that was being stuck, well, I wouldn't mind it.

At last I turned off my flashlight and looked up into the night sky. Stars everywhere, many more and much more beautiful than they are at home. At home the stars have to compete with the streetlights and the house lights. But up here, they shine all by themselves. I love the stars.

The stars reminded me how big and mighty God is and how He could help me through any trouble I might have, no matter how big.

14 Ray's Advice

Eyes closed, hands clasped behind my head, I basked on my Mickey Mouse towel by the pool. It was morning free time, and I was tanning my body in eighty-five degrees of mountain sun. This was definitely the life. Guys were shouting in the pool. Occasionally a drop of water would come my way and startle me.

I opened my eyes and looked up at the tops of the pine trees that towered above me. Birds flew in and out among the lower branches of the trees. Frankly, I was jealous.

Birds, I decided, have the life. Their bodies are designed to eat worms. Fat juicy worms that are just lying around, waiting. Birds can fly anywhere they want to go. If they want to be at camp, then fine, they go to camp. If they want to sit on a telephone wire, no one stops them. If a bird ditched campfire and was overheard talking to his mother on the phone, no one would care.

I knew—though I wished there was a way out—that I was going to have to tell someone about Stuart's call.

But who? Could I write a message on a napkin at lunch and pass it to Stuart?

Stuart, the note would say, *I know everything. It's time to come clean.*

No, I decided, that would never work. He might just throw the note away and go on with his life.

Maybe I should talk to Cowboy Joe. After all, he was a reform school principal, and he was used to dealing with situations far worse than unauthorized phone calls. Or what about going directly to the Trail Boss, since it was his office that had been used for the call?

All these thoughts collided in a big mess inside my brain. I tried to think of a way out. Maybe, under the influence of the six peanut butter s'mores, I had hallucinated the entire scene.

But no, every word Stuart had said was clearly etched in my memory. Particularly the way he had told his mom he could help out if he were at home. Why? Why did he need to help out if his grandma was so rich?

Splash! I was soaking wet. My towel was soaking wet.

"Come on, Jenkins! We're doing relays."

"Okay, okay," I said. So much for my tan. I hung my towel over the fence to dry and jumped into the pool. Teams were chosen and, after much shouting, we decided to do a cannon-ball-roller relay. I was first in my line. Jared Spence, our resident archery expert, was behind me.

"Do you swim as well as you shoot?" I asked.

"Naturally," he said.

The lifeguard blew his whistle, and I cannonballed into the water. As I came up for air, I laid my body crosswise in the water and began rolling to the far end of the pool. This included quite a lot of thrashing about and gulping of water. After an eternity, I made it to the other end, hauled myself out and shouted "Go!" That was the signal for Jared to take a splash.

True to his word, he rolled like an expert. I cheered him on the whole way. Together we shouted "Go" when he pulled himself out of the pool, dripping and laughing.

"Where is Robin Hood?" I asked him. Robin hadn't been at archery that morning. I figured someone would have told Jared why.

"Robin Hood?"

"You know, the kid who wanted to show you how to shoot yesterday."

"Oh, him. He switched to horseback riding."

I wondered if his parents would mind the extra expense. I know what my dad would have said.

"So," I could just hear Dad saying, "you made a fool of yourself by pretending to be a big shot, huh? You can just stick it out, Arb. Maybe you'll learn something."

We won the first relay, but we lost the second, which was a swan-dive-feet-first-sculling race. After that, I was dead beat. I laid totally flat on my still-damp towel and closed my eyes.

"What's wrong, Arb?" I squinted open one eye. It was Ray.

"I'm exhausted, that's what," I said.

"Can't fool me, buddy," he said. "Something's wrong. Cough it up."

I coughed. Ray didn't laugh.

"Okay, okay," I said. "I'll tell you, if you'll promise not to say anything to anyone."

"Promise," said Ray. He unrolled his towel and sat down on it.

I sighed. There was no getting around it now. Ray would sit there until I told him everything.

"I was sick last night from eating six peanut butter s'mores—"

"Peanut butter s'mores!" Ray shouted. "What a great idea! What's so bad about that?"

"Be quiet, Ray," I said. "I am trying to tell you something important."

"Sorry."

I told him the whole story. Every word of Stuart's conversation and the background stuff, like Stuart's bad attitude, the four-eyes comment, and how he didn't fit in with the guys, except that he was a great athlete, and so on.

"So the question is—?" he said.

"The question is, what am I going to do about it?"

"Nope. The question is, do you want me to come with you to confront Stuart?"

"Confront him?"

"Yes, Arb." He spoke like a parent speaking to a naughty child. "And you know it. Remember what Pastor says about confronting your brother when he has offended you."

"Ah ha!" I said. "Stuart is not saved, so he's not my Christian brother." I looked at Ray in triumph. This, surely, was the way out of my dilemma. I could forget about it and go on with my life. What did I care, anyway, whether Stuart snuck away from campfire? What did it matter to me if he called his mom every night for two weeks?

"That doesn't matter one bit," Ray said. But he'd hesitated, so I pressed the point.

"Why doesn't it matter?" I asked. I wanted a good reason, now that I'd decided to toss the entire memory out of my mind and enjoy the next week and a half of camp free from nagging thoughts. If the Trail Boss had locked his office door instead of leaving it wide open to any kid who happened to come by, this would never have happened.

I smiled. That was it. It was the Trail Boss's fault. He ought to know better than to leave his door unlocked when homesick kids were wandering around looking for a way to call their moms.

I'll bet Cowboy Brian didn't leave his office unlocked with the welcome mat out to anyone who wanted a few bandages or some aspirin, I thought. I sighed, lay back on Mickey Mouse's damp ears, and closed my eyes.

"Arby," said Ray.

I opened my eyes.

"Can't think of a reason, can you?" I said.

"Look here, Arby," Ray said. "Stuart is lying by making people think he's at campfire when he's not. He needs to be at campfire. He's not saved, right? That's one thing. The other thing is, he's stealing by putting long-distance calls on the camp phone bill. You can't just sit there and not do something."

Oh. Lying and stealing. I hadn't thought of it that way before. It seemed strange that calling your own mother could be lying and stealing, but there it was. Ray was right.

I sighed. "Okay, Ray. I'll talk to him after lunch."

"Want me to come with you?" he asked.

"No, I can do it."

15 Confrontation

At lunch time, Cowboy Joe appeared with a smile that took up his whole face.

"Hey, boys," he said. "Let's take a walk!"

"A walk?" I asked. "It's lunch time, isn't it?"

"Yeah," said several boys, "it's lunch time."

"That's right, cowpokes," said the principal-turned-counselor. "And like I always say, 'A good walk builds a man's appetite.' We're taking a picnic lunch, just the Mighty Mustangs."

"Yea!"

We said "Yea" because we did not understand that when you take a hike out of camp with a picnic lunch, everyone has to carry something.

Stuart and I got stuck carrying the drinks. We each carried two two-liter bottles of soda pop. These got heavier as we walked along. After a little while my arms ached and I wished I had a wheelbarrow to cart them in. I tried carrying my bottles on one arm to give the other arm a rest. I tried holding them on my shoulders. Nothing helped. After a while, Stuart and I were lagging behind the other boys.

Oh boy, I thought, *this is it.* I said a short prayer for boldness and launched into my speech, which didn't turn out long or as brilliant as I had planned.

"I heard you talking to your mom last night, Stuart," I said.

Stuart stopped in his tracks and put the soda pop down on the path. "So?" he asked loudly. "So what? What of it? What are you going to do about it?"

I stopped walking and looked back at him. This wasn't exactly the reaction I had expected. "Well," I said, "I don't want to do anything about it. But you're going to have to."

"What?" said Stuart. "What am I going to have to do about it, huh, Jenkins?"

His voice got louder and I had the feeling he wanted to punch me. I pictured myself lying prone and bleeding with my head propped up on a two-liter bottle of Dr. Pepper.

"Come on, Stuart," I said. "We need to get to the picnic."

Stuart picked up his bottles and glared at me. He didn't move.

I tried again. "Look, it's wrong for you to ditch campfire. It's wrong to make telephone calls because it's against the rules."

"Fine, Four-Eyes," Stuart shouted. "Go ahead and tell. Just be a tattletale."

That four-eyes comment really hurt. I stood my ground and hoped I wouldn't cry. "I am not a tattletale," I said. "You are the person who needs to go tell. You need to go to the Trail Boss or Cowboy Joe and apologize for what you've done and promise not to do it again. They're going to find out anyway."

"How?" asked Stuart. "I thought you said you weren't going to tell."

"Whether I tell or not, they'll still find out," I said. "When the telephone bill comes in, the Trail Boss will figure it out. It'll be there in black and white."

"So, Mr. Know-It-All," Stuart said. "I'll bet you don't know anything about telephone bills, do you? I bet you've never even seen one, have you?"

"No."

"Well, I've seen plenty of bills," said Stuart. "And if I was home instead of stuck up here at this stupid camp, I could be working to help my mom pay the bills instead of talking to dumb kids like you in the middle of nowhere."

"Why should you need to help out? From what you've said, your grandma is made of money."

"That's all you know," Stuart said. "Why don't you just mind your own business? Maybe not everybody's life is peaches and cream like yours. Maybe some people have problems, okay?"

"Stuart," I said. "That's not the point. I'm sorry about your problems, really I am. But you've got to tell the Trail Boss the truth. I'm sure he would let you call your mom if you need to talk to her."

"Just forget about it, Arby," said Stuart. "Why don't you just be a little Mr. Goody-Goody and mind your own business and leave me alone?"

"It is my business."

"In what way?"

"Look," I said. I was getting angry now, but I was trying to control my spirit like my dad tells me to. "You have broken the rules. I saw and heard you do it. If you don't tell, I'm going to have to tell. That's just the way it is."

"Fine," said Stuart. "Go ahead and tell. They'll pack me up and send me home which is where I want to be anyway. Then I won't have to be here in a dumb covered wagon with a bunch of dumb Christians who think they're better than everybody else."

Now that made me mad. I really wanted to punch him.

"Stop it," I said. "Nobody has said they're better than you. A Christian is someone who has been forgiven of his sins.

Because his sins are forgiven, he can go to heaven. It's trusting Christ, not being better than everyone, that counts."

I took a deep breath. My whole body was trembling. This was the biggest witness I had ever given. I wondered if it counted as witnessing since I'd been so mad. I waited for Stuart's reaction

But he didn't react. He just stood there and looked at me. I didn't know what to do. I couldn't think of anything new to say, so I said something I had already said.

"You tell, or I tell, Stuart. It's that simple. Come on, let's get to the picnic."

We picked up the soda pop and walked the rest of the way to the clearing. It was the same place we'd had superdeluxe s'mores the night before. Neither of us spoke.

It seemed like years had passed since last night. I felt like I'd aged, and I wondered if my hair was still brown, or if it had started turning gray.

"There you are at last!" called Cowboy Joe when Stuart and I finally arrived at the fire ring. The fire was already blazing, and all the other guys had their skewers.

I started thinking about what had happened and began roasting my hot dog. It was in flames before I noticed that anything was wrong. Completely black, it fell apart into the fire when I touched it with another stick. I asked Cowboy Joe for another hot dog, but there weren't any more. I put mustard on my bun and munched it slowly as I watched the fire die.

16 All Wet

I got a letter from Mom that afternoon. A letter from home reminded me that I would live through all the vicissitudes of camp. I would eventually get home. Not that I didn't like camp. Camp was great, and I was glad I had been able to come at last.

It was the little things that were happening to me—nightmares, rude kids—that were making it hard. So it was wonderful, that Wednesday, to get a letter from my mom.

Dear Arby,

I hope you are having fun at camp. Is Ray in your wagon? Is the food good? Are you wearing your coat?

I am in Cincinnati getting Grandma packed up and ready to move. She has so many things! She is a little sad to be leaving her house, but she knows it's best for everyone. I'm sad too. This is the house I grew up in, you know. I pray often that she will take the move well and that she will adjust easily to life at our house.

I talked with Dad yesterday. Dell has moved his things into your room. You may not recognize the place. Thanks for having such a good attitude about all these changes.

I have enclosed five dollars. I hope you can get a nice souvenir. See you in a few days.

Love,

Mom

Not sure I'd recognize my own room. Oh no, I thought. The piles of clothes. The posters of basketball players. The aquarium he'd dug out of someone's trash—to keep snails in. I decided to get a paper route so I could help with the addition we would have to build. Or maybe I could move into the garage. My mattress would fit between the front of the car and the washing machine. It would be a snug fit—and plenty cold—but worth it.

I sat on my bunk and wrote a letter back to my mom. It was about time, really. My mom had packed five stamped envelopes addressed to her in my suitcase. Talk about a big hint that I was supposed to write letters home. Up til now, I hadn't written even one. But I had a few minutes now before canoeing class, so I wrote my mom a letter.

Dear Mom,

Thanks for your letter. Camp is fun. My counselor is Cowboy Joe. He is a principul in his real job, so you know I'm being good. The food is okay, but not like home. Ray is in a different wagon. I'm taking archery and canoeing. So far I haven't fallen in the lake. Thank you for the $5. Maybe I will buy a belt buckle.

Love,

Arby

P.S. Tell Dell I've got a great modification for chess.

For canoeing class, we rode in the counselors' cars to the lake that was a couple of miles up the road. The canoes were lashed to the tops of the cars, and the paddles and life jackets were stowed in the trunks.

The lake was beautiful, surrounded by mountains, and shining in the sunlight. One of the counselors passed around a bottle of sunscreen, and I rubbed some on my face.

Cowboy Joe was in charge of this class, which made me glad. Yesterday had been our first trip to the lake, so we knew already who our canoe partners were, and we'd learned the basics of canoeing. At least enough to get us to the middle of the lake and paddling around.

There were three boys in my canoe: me, Tom from Pinto Place, and Doug from Old Paint. Doug is also in my class at school and goes to my church.

We pushed off and paddled to the center of the lake. We all had life jackets on, of course, which made things a little bit hotter and awkward, but it wasn't bad.

"How's Old Paint, Doug?" I asked.

"It's great."

That was all he said. We sat out there in the middle of the lake, not paddling, for a while. We were soaking up the sun and admiring the scenery.

I looked over at another canoe with three guys in it who were paddling furiously and getting nowhere. One of the guys was Ray.

"Look at Ray's canoe!" I said.

We looked over at them splashing at the water with their paddles. I laughed and decided to give them some expert advice, since I had been an ace canoeist now for two whole days.

I stood up in the canoe to shout instructions. "Hey, you guys! You've got to—"

That was as far as I got before our canoe tipped over. I dimly heard my canoe-mates shouting "Uh oh!" as I plunged beneath the surface of the lake.

My first thought—other than the humiliation of it all—was my glasses. Then Dell's hat. I reached for my face with one hand and my head with the other. The glasses were there. What a relief. The hat was not. Uh oh, I thought. I've drowned Dell's hat. He'll never forgive me.

We popped up to the surface quickly, thanks to our life jackets, then we held on to the bottom of the upside-down canoe. Cowboy Joe rowed over and rescued us. My glasses were wet, and I couldn't dry them because my shirt was wet. The world, therefore, looked blurred and watery.

"You might as well just stay in the canoe and get some sun," said Cowboy Joe. "It's the best way to get dry." He paddled around, picking up my brother's wet hat and collecting our paddles, which floated on the water.

I took a lot of teasing over this. One kid in Ray's canoe shouted, "Hey, expert, how's the water?" I couldn't blame him. I felt small and foolish.

"You going to teach the class tomorrow?" asked Doug.

I splashed him with my paddle.

The worst thing about being all wet was the soaked jeans. Anyone who's ever sat around in wet jeans knows they are heavy and uncomfortable. And of course they would dry only on the side that faced the sun, which was the top side.

So, when it was time to get out of the canoes and get back into the cars, the front of my jeans and the rest of my clothes were dry, while the back side of the jeans were still wet. We sat on towels in the car. Then, the minute we got back to camp, we bolted for our wagons.

When I ran up the ladder into my wagon, I almost tripped over Stuart who was coming out.

"So did you tattle yet?" he asked.

"Huh?" My concern at the moment was getting into dry pants.

"Did you go rat on me to Cowboy Joe?"

"Oh," I said. "No, I didn't. I figured I'd give you some time."

I pushed past him. The good thing was, Stuart had been thinking about what I'd said earlier. Whether he understood that he'd done something wrong, I didn't know.

I told him how I'd managed to dump a whole canoe load of kids into the lake. I'd hoped he would laugh at that, but he didn't.

"Arby," Stuart said, "would you like to call with me tonight?"

"What?" I asked. I was astonished.

"Well, first of all, anyone can see that you're homesick like I am."

"A little," I said, "but it's getting better. I got a letter from my mom today."

I reached into my wet pocket and pulled out the soggy letter.

"All you need to do is sneak away from campfire with me, and we'll both call home. You can talk with your mom, and I can call mine. We'll be back at campfire before anyone notices we're gone."

All I could think of was Jesus saying to Peter, "Get thee behind me, Satan," but, honestly, I couldn't very well have said that to Stuart. He knew if I called home, he wouldn't have to worry about me ratting on him to the counselors.

"Not for a million bucks," I said. "Not for a billion. Come on, I'll go with you to talk to Cowboy Joe. You've got to, you know."

"Oh, I do, do I?"

"Yes." I was tired of this conversation.

I changed my clothes without saying anything more to Stuart. I got my soggy five-dollar bill out of my jeans pocket and unfolded the soggy letter, now soaked and smeared. All I could read now was the postmark on the envelope: Cincinnati, Ohio.

"Stuart," I said, "what's wrong at home?"

From the look on his face I thought he was trying to figure out whether to trust me. I was pretty sure he wouldn't. I was right.

"None of your business. Everything's fine."

17 Hide-and-Seek

At dinner we Mighty Mustangs did our wagon cheer. During each meal, one wagon group would do a cheer for their wagon. Now it was our turn.

We had just finished our salads. Before we could start on our hamburgers, Cowboy Joe said, "Okay, boys. Now." We stood.

Drew said, "One, two, ready, go!" and we launched into our cheer as loud as we could shout.

Mustangs! Mustangs! Leaders of the Pack!
Mustangs! Mustangs! Never looking back!
Fierce in every challenge!
Calm against each foe!
Mustangs! Mustangs! Go! Go! Go!

Then we shouted, "Yea, Mighty Mustangs!" and sat down and finished our dinners.

It made us giddy to have yelled in the dining hall in front of the whole camp. I noticed my hands shaking as I squirted mustard onto my hamburger bun.

Stuart sat next to me at dinner. As I took a huge bite of hamburger, he whispered to me. "I'm out of here."

"Wha—?" I couldn't form a question. My mouth was too full.

"Like I said, I'm history."

I didn't know what he meant. Did he think I'd told Cowboy Joe about the phone calls? I hadn't. I figured I'd tell him tonight if Stuart hadn't said anything by then.

"History?" I asked with my mouth still very full.

"Yeah," he said. "I called my mom. She said she'd come get me away from here."

I could tell by his tone of voice this was a lie. "Why, Stuart?" I whispered. "Do you really hate camp that much? Is it that bad?"

"It's the God stuff," he said. "I can't stand it."

"Oh." I didn't know what else to say.

When song time was over, the Trail Boss announced the evening's activities. "Okay, cowpokes, here's the scoop for tonight. Now listen up! I think you're going to enjoy this one. It's our famous Super-Hide-and-Seek-Make-Your-Own-Sundae Night! The game will start as soon as it's dark. You'll need your coats and flashlights. Then, after the game, we'll have ice-cream sundaes!"

The dining hall went wild at this announcement. There was the usual cheering and stomping of feet and banging on tables. They divided us into the Red Team and the Blue Team for the hide-and-seek game. The game would have two rounds. In the first round, the Blues would hide until the Reds had found all of them. Then, in the second round, the Reds would hide until the Blues found them. After the second round, we would all come back to the dining room, where long tables would be set up with the ingredients for make-your-own ice-cream sundaes.

I was glad Stuart was not on my team. I didn't believe for one minute that his mom was coming to get him. And I was angry at him for not confessing yet, but at the same time I felt sorry for whatever it was at home that was so bad. I also couldn't figure out whether I was happy or sad that all the "God stuff" as he called it was getting to him. And what did he mean by "I'm out of here"?

Dan, Mike, and I were on the Blues. Stuart and Drew were Reds. That meant that I was on the first team to hide. During the second round, the Reds would hide and we Blues would go out looking for them. Points would be awarded for the number of hiders each seeker caught. I determined first of all not to be caught by any old Red team member, and second, to find as many Reds as I could when it was my turn to look.

We had to have our coats put on and zipped up in order to receive our red or blue arm band. We also had to show that we had a working flashlight.

"Playing games in the dark is fun, boys," the Trail Boss had said, "but it's important to be well-equipped."

The only hide-and-seek I'd ever played—other than at school during recess—was at home with the neighborhood kids. We used to mark off the limits and then play until the streetlights came on. After that, we had to go inside, so that was the end of the game.

As soon as everyone had an arm band, the Trail Boss explained the outer limits we could use for the game.

"You can hide anywhere in camp, but not inside any building," he said. "You may not go past the wagon train to the north or the dining hall to the south. The campfire is the western limit, and the road is the eastern limit. Is everyone clear on the boundaries?"

Everyone was clear. Everyone was ready. I could see several people huddled together, no doubt talking about good hiding places, but I already had my place in mind. I intended to sit there until I heard the shout "Ollie Ollie Oxen; free, free, free!" When the other team shouted this, it meant that anyone who hadn't been found was a winner and could come out without being caught.

The whistle blew, and the Red team lay flat on the ground with their arms covering their heads so they couldn't watch any of the Blues hide.

The Trail Boss started them counting, "One," he shouted, "two!"

I took off. I ran straight for the hedge that grew along the back side of the office building. I had thought of this hedge immediately when the Trail Boss mentioned the hide-and-seek game. I was sure I could get into it and hide successfully without being found.

Nobody was around the hedge, and I had plenty of time to wiggle my way into it without being seen. It took a while and scratched me up a good bit, but it was worth it.

I was right. No one came anywhere near. I heard people in the distance shouting, "I see you! You're caught!" and people who had been caught shouting, "Ah, too bad," but no one came close to me.

So there I was, stuck in a hedge. I had cut my hands and feet and probably torn my jacket for the glory of my team. I sat in the hedge a long time, and at last I began to wonder if the call "Ollie Ollie Oxen; free, free, free!" had been sounded, and if it hadn't, whether it would be best to just get out of here, if I could.

As I was pondering this thought and wondering if I'd be stuck in the hedge all night and whether anyone would notice I was missing, I heard someone coming.

A person—a boy about my size—walked slowly past me. It was Stuart. In a moment I realized that he was not searching for Blue team members. He had his red arm band on, but he was looking over his shoulder as if he was worried that someone might be following him. He walked toward the trees that led out of the camp.

"I'm out of here," he had said at dinner. Was he running away from camp? A sick feeling grew in my stomach. I felt suddenly responsible for Stuart, and I knew that—as awful and dangerous as it sounded—I had to follow him.

I eased myself out of the hedge and checked my flashlight to make sure it worked. Then, I took off after Stuart as quietly and quickly as I could go.

I knew that if he was trying to run away, it would be best if he didn't hear anything behind him that might scare him. He was fast, but he was unused to the woods. He crashed loudly through the trees.

Dad had taken me camping many times. He'd taught me about leaving landmarks along a trail so that I wouldn't get lost. I knew I had to do this, even if it meant losing Stuart. I figured my dad would kill me if I got lost in the woods and froze to death.

I stopped and reached for my pocketknife. I cut my arm band into strips and tied a strip to a branch every so often. Since Stuart was thrashing up a trail, it wouldn't be hard to find my way back, but you never know. Best to follow Dad's advice.

Stuart jogged away at a steady pace. I pushed myself to keep up, but I knew I couldn't do it forever. Stuart was a natural athlete, and I, well, I was more of a Monopoly man myself. I could see the light of his flashlight ahead. The moon was bright, also, which helped a great deal. It meant I could save the batteries in my flashlight.

I could hear Stuart's heavy breathing. I worked hard at taking shallow breaths so he wouldn't hear me. He didn't turn around. There was no reason for him to think he'd been followed. No one had been around when he left the camp boundaries. No one but a kid stuffed inside a hedge.

After what seemed like hours, Stuart finally stopped and looked around. I stepped behind a tree and breathed as quietly as I could. The pounding of my heart echoed through the forest, but Stuart apparently couldn't hear it. Maybe he could only hear his own.

I was tired, exhausted in fact, and more than a little bit afraid. And I had run out of strips of blue arm band to hang on the trees.

The wind picked up now, and the sound of it whooshing through the trees was terrifying. What in the world had I done? Who did I think I was to go tromping after Stuart Baltz, the world's all-time creepy camper?

I peeked around my tree and saw Stuart. He had sat down at the base of a large pine and was resting his back against it. Out here he didn't look like a creep. He looked like a little kid who was lost in the woods and needed help.

I wondered how long we'd be here before help came. Probably no one would even notice we were gone until lights out. How long until lights out, I wondered.

When we'd left camp, it had been only the first round of Hide-and-Seek. True, I'd thought I was in the hedge for an eternity, but a few minutes crammed in that jabby place would feel like forever. The more I thought about it, the more I realized that I had probably been inside the hedge no more than five minutes when Stuart went by.

Surely the first round would go half an hour or more, and then the second round would take at least that long. No one would notice that two boys were missing.

Then after the game, there was the ice-cream feed. Oh, I was mad at Stuart for making me miss that. The ice-cream party would go on for at least an hour, and no one would take roll there.

All my figuring got me to this conclusion: no one would look for us for at least two hours. Then they would think, since both Stuart and I were missing, that we were off talking somewhere.

I was getting worried. If Cowboy Joe thought I was witnessing to Stuart, he might not be concerned if we weren't back by lights out, which was ten-thirty. It might be eleven or even later before Cowboy Joe decided to look for us.

I had no idea what time it was. My watch was sitting safe and sound on my dresser at home, where I had put it Sunday night. I had left it in plain sight so that I wouldn't forget to wear it to camp.

Stuart got up from the ground and started off again, slower this time. I stayed well behind him, out of his vision and hearing. I could tell he was afraid by the way he flashed his light up and around in front of him. Every so often he stopped to listen. An owl hooted, and there were little skittering noises, but nothing awful. No growls or roars.

My dad is the great woodsman in my family, but even I knew enough to know that a couple of junior high boys wandering in the woods in the middle of the night with no food and no extra batteries is not the safest thing in the world. The fact was, we were far from camp and totally lost.

Stuart stopped and started every few yards. He seemed confused and frightened. He turned and looked back the way we'd come, but I flatted myself against a tree and he didn't see me.

Then he sat down and started talking to himself out loud. The sound of a human voice startled me. I crouched behind a tree and listened.

"Dumb Jenkins kid," he said. "Why can't he keep his nose out of my business?"

After a while he said, "Dumb, stupid camp. Everything is God and Jesus and dedicating your life. And getting saved."

He picked up a pine cone and threw it hard at the tree opposite to him. It broke in pieces and rolled along the ground.

It was enough for me to know that he was not just running away from camp. He was running away from God. It reminded me of Jonah. Then I thought that if he was Jonah, that made me the whale. It remained to be seen whether I'd save him from drowning, although I must admit I was ready to spit him up on the shore.

Suddenly the wind whipped through the treetops. Stuart gave a little scream. The sound of the wind in the trees on a mountain when you're camping with your family is one thing. The wind in the trees when you're lost and know that no one is going to be looking for you for hours is something else entirely.

Stuart slid to the ground again. He shone his flashlight around him. It silhouetted the trees, and I think that scared him more than just sitting in the darkness. He turned the flashlight off.

I fought the urge to tell him I was there. I was still afraid that if he knew I had followed him he would get mad and maybe punch me. Stuart could beat me up easily and then leave me to rot on the forest floor. Not a pretty picture.

So, I couldn't tell Stuart yet that I was there. I would have to wait a little while longer.

It was at this point that I looked up into the tree I was hiding behind. It had good branches. I wondered if I could climb it and signal Ray with my flashlight. Not that I knew which direction to face, and not that anyone would see my signals if I did face the right direction.

Even if they did see them, would any of them know enough Morse code to recognize a distress signal? Or would they be smart enough, even if they didn't know Morse code, to follow a light they could barely see when they knew two of their kids were lost?

If they even knew we were lost.

18 The Flashlight Code

At least I could try climbing the tree, I decided. Then I'd find out if I could see anything from higher up. The problem was that the lowest branch was a couple of feet above my head. I would have to jump for it. And I would have to catch the branch on the first try or Stuart would hear me crash to the ground. Even just catching onto the branch and pulling myself up would make some noise, but the wind was fairly loud and might cover for me. Maybe Stuart wouldn't be too alarmed by the sound of a moving branch.

I grabbed the branch on my first try and hauled myself up onto it. I was breathing hard over this feat and wished someone had seen me accomplish it. If I lived through the night, I would add this to my list of things to remember.

Apparently, Stuart hadn't heard me swinging into the tree. From my new elevated position, I could look down and see him sitting at the base of a tree about three trees off, with his chin resting on his knees. He was swinging his flashlight from side to side as if he were warding off enemies with a sword.

Up in the tree, I realized that trying to go higher was going to do me no good. The trees around me were all as tall as my tree, and I would have to get to the very top before I would have any vantage point from which to signal anyone. I didn't need a college degree to know that it would be foolish to try climbing to the top of a tall tree in the middle of the night when I was lost in the woods.

I was stuck in the tree. I couldn't go up and I couldn't come down. If I dropped down to the ground, Stuart would hear me.

Thus, I was sitting not too comfortably on the branch of a tree when Stuart started talking to himself again. I think he was talking out loud just to hear his own voice. I didn't blame him. It was scary out here.

"Great, Baltz," he said to himself, "just get lost in the mountains. That'll really help Mom out."

What happened next surprised me.

"Okay, God," Stuart said. "I'm lost in the woods now."

I prayed silently, "Please God, help me to help Stuart."

He stood up suddenly and shouted "Help, Help!"

I kept still.

Then he sat down again against the tree trunk. "Fine, God," he said. "Just leave me here to rot. Grandma says you watch over her because she's your child. I wish you would watch over me too."

"Stuart," I said, from my perch in the tree, "it's going to be okay."

He jumped up and shined his flashlight around wildly. Finally, he caught me on my branch with the light.

"Jenkins!" he shouted. "I thought you were God!"

"Not hardly," I said.

I made up my mind all of a sudden and decided to jump on down. I fell with a thud. "Aahh! My ankle!"

"Great, Tarzan," he said. He helped me up and then asked, "You okay? How did you find me?"

"I followed you all the way," I said.

"You mean you've been with me the whole time?"

"Yep." I hobbled over to where he'd been sitting before and sat down. I pulled up the leg of my pants. My ankle was already swelling. I wondered if I'd broken it trying to be a hero.

"I saw you go past the hedge where I was hiding for hide-and-seek," I said, "I was worried you were running away, so I followed you."

Stuart stared at me for a long time.

"Thanks, Arby."

After another minute he said, "We're lost."

"True," I said, "but it's not hopeless."

I told him about my arm band landmarks, which probably no one would ever find, and then I told him about our best hope: the flashlights.

"What we need to do, Stuart, is to find a high place where I can signal Ray with my signaler."

"What's a signaler?"

I showed him how the flashlight worked and told him about the signalman's club, and how Ray and I flashed Morse code signals to each other from our rooftops. I talked fast, in what I hoped was a cheerful tone, to make him think I was in control of the situation and unafraid.

We started walking. Well, actually, Stuart started walking and I started hobbling. We had come up a fairly steep incline, so I figured if we could get a little higher up, we might find a clearing. Then I could signal and hope someone would see it. I showed Stuart how to use the flashlight to look all around, not just at the ground in front of us.

After a few minutes, we saw a large rock, off to the right and above us. It took me quite a while to get up close to it. Stuart steadied me. Then I boosted him up to the top of the rock.

"What can you see?" I asked.

"I can see some lights, Arb! I can see lights down there!"

Wonderful news. Stuart reached down and hauled me up. My ankle throbbed, but I leaned on Stuart and felt steady enough to stand. Stuart flashed his flashlight all over the place.

"Relax, Stuart," I said. "Let's make a plan."

The plan was to use the signaler to flash an S O S every couple of minutes. We couldn't just turn our lights on and shine them around. They might not attract attention and the batteries would run down. But an S O S would attract the attention of anyone who happened to see it. And almost anyone, I was sure, would understand an S O S. If they saw it, that is.

We sat down on the rock. I flashed an S O S every couple of minutes for what seemed like forever. Hours perhaps. Some of the lights below us went out. The air grew colder. We pulled our coats tighter around us. My ankle swelled and I had to take my shoe off. I longed for my watch and began to wonder if we were going to be stuck up on this rock all night. That was not the kind of adventure I wanted. And besides, we'd still be lost in the morning.

"Hey, Arby," Stuart said, "how come you waited so long to tell me you were there?"

"I was afraid you'd beat me up."

"Oh. Good point."

After that, Stuart and I began to talk. In between S O S's, I told him about Grandma Parsons coming to live with us. I told him I was worried about living in the same room with Dell. He told me about his Grandma Ellie who played the organ. I asked him why he never came to church with her, and he said he hadn't been interested in "all that Christian stuff."

"Hadn't been?" I asked. "Does that mean you might be more interested now?"

"Tell me this, Jenkins," he said. "Why did you follow me?"

"I was afraid you'd get lost. I didn't want you to be lost."

"Thanks, Arby."

I gave Stuart the signaler and showed him how to flash S O S: three short flashes, three long flashes, three short flashes. This is the universal distress signal, and I was hopeful that if it was not actually known universally it would at least be known by whoever might see it down below.

"Look up! Look up!" I shouted, jumping up. Then I immediately shouted "Ouch!" because I had jumped on my hurt ankle. I wavered on the rock, but Stuart caught me and helped me sit down.

"What are you shouting about, Arby?" asked Stuart.

"Well," I said, "it occurs to me that anyone who is looking for us around camp will never dream of looking way up here. That's why I shouted 'Look up!' "

"If they even know we're gone," said Stuart.

"They know," I said, not convinced. In fact, I was sure no one knew where we were. I needed to pray.

"Stuart," I said, "I am going to pray."

"Good," he said. "Pray away."

"Dear Heavenly Father," I prayed, "please help us because we are lost. We need you to send someone to find us. We need someone to see our distress signal. We need to be saved. In Jesus' name, Amen."

We sat on our rock, signaling and talking, Stuart and I. He told me, at last, about his home problems. His father had left home when Stuart was a baby. The last time he'd seen him,

Stuart had been two years old. For several years Stuart's mom had been able to keep the house, but recently she had lost her job, so Stuart and his mom had had to move in with Mrs. Stinson, his Grandma Ellie.

"What does your mom do for work now?" I asked.

"She's a waitress at Cook's," he said.

"We love Cook's," I said. "They have the best shrimp."

"Now you're talking," said Stuart, suddenly animated. "Mom brings it home sometimes in a Styrofoam tray."

The shrimp business got Stuart talking. He told me about his school and his friends back at the old house, and how hard it was to leave the neighborhood, and how upset he was with his father for leaving them.

"What do you know about him?" I asked.

"He lied to my mom. He left me. And he was a Christian, like you."

Oh. "I don't get it," I said. "How can a man be a follower of Jesus and leave his family?"

"That's my question," he said.

We sat there in silence, flashing the light every few minutes. I had a lot of questions and no answers.

"You never see him?" I asked.

"Never," he said. "Except in pictures. Mom still has her wedding pictures. One night when I couldn't sleep, I went to the kitchen to get something to eat. Mom was in the living room. She was sitting on the couch, looking through her wedding pictures and crying. I sat down beside her and cried too. And then I went to bed because I didn't know what to say to make it any better."

S O S, I flashed. S O S. S O S.

"Stuart," I said, "I'm sorry."

"Thanks," he said. Then suddenly, "Arby! Look!"

There it was, plain as day, a long flash. An answering flash!

Stuart pulled me up and starting doing a sort of jig.

"Stop it, Stuart, I have to read the signal!" I pulled away from him, balanced on my good foot, and focused on the light.

It was Ray all right. His message was this: "Arby, are you hurt?"

I read the message out loud for Stuart's benefit. Then I took the signaler back from him and signaled: "Twisted my ankle. Very cold. Send help."

I translated for Stuart as I signaled.

"Cool," said Stuart. "This is awesome."

Ray replied: "What's your location?"

I flashed: "Top of a large rock. We left from behind office building. Blue pieces of arm band on trees. Follow thrashed-up trail. Stuart's an amateur."

I laughed as I signaled this.

"Hey," said Stuart, "what're you laughing at?"

"Never mind," I said. "I'll tell you later."

Ray signaled: "Trail Boss and Cowboy Brian coming. What happened?"

"Stuart ran away. I think he will be okay now. We had a talk."

"Good work, Arb. Why don't you make some noise so they can hear you?"

This was a good idea. I told Stuart that Ray had suggested we make some noise. We had come a good long way, and I figured it would take the Trail Boss and Cowboy Brian some time to find us. Making noise would be comforting, so we stood on the rock and shouted our cheer:

Mustangs! Mustangs! Leaders of the Pack!
Mustangs! Mustangs! Never looking Back!
Fierce in every challenge!
Calm against each foe!
Mustangs! Mustangs! Go! Go! Go!

We shouted this cheer about ten times at the top of our lungs. Then Stuart got quiet and sat down on the rock with his head in his hands.

"What's wrong, Stuart?" I asked.

"They'll send me home."

"They won't send you home," I said.

"They will too send me home," he said. "Look what I've done. I've made stolen phone calls for one thing. I've run away from camp for another, and I've broken your ankle."

"You didn't break my ankle," I said. "I broke my own ankle playing Tarzan."

"It was my fault. They'll send me home."

He looked up at me. "I don't want to go home. I want to stay here." He paused. "Maybe I can learn some things about God."

I sat down next to him.

"They won't send you home," I said.

19 In the Bag

It wasn't too long before we heard the Trail Boss and Cowboy Brian calling our names.

"Over here! Up on the rock!" we shouted.

My ankle hurt badly now, and I couldn't even stand. As the men came in sight, Stuart crouched behind me as if he were trying to hide.

Cowboy Brian was right behind the Trail Boss, and he was carrying a first-aid kit under one arm and a blanket under the other. The Trail Boss had a blanket in one arm and a heavy-duty flashlight in the other.

"Here we are!" I shouted. Stuart was not shouting anymore.

Cowboy Brian hopped up onto the rock and took a look at my ankle. Then he wrapped it up tightly with an Ace bandage. He helped me stand up, and I found I could walk if I leaned on him. He also wrapped a blanket around me. That's when I realized I was shivering.

While Cowboy Brian attended to me, the Trail Boss talked to Stuart. I listened, even though I knew better than to eavesdrop on other people's conversations.

"You okay, Stuart?"

"Yes," said Stuart. "I'm sorry, Trail Boss. Are you going to send me home?"

"Do you want to go home?" asked the Trail Boss.

"No," said Stuart. "But I stole the calls and ditched campfire and broke Arby's ankle and—"

"Stole calls?" said the Trail Boss.

Stuart came clean. He told everything. I stopped pretending I wasn't listening and watched the Trail Boss's face. It was stern, like my dad's when he's about to bring the curtain down on some stupid thing I've done.

"So, I'm sorry, Trail Boss, and I want to stay. Arby showed me that Christians aren't all bad."

The Trail Boss looked up at me.

"It's his dad," I said.

So Stuart told about his dad while Cowboy Brian looked him over and wrapped him in a blanket.

"Baltz," the Trail Boss said when Stuart had finished his story.

"Yes, sir?"

"You ready for another week of camp?"

"Yes, sir!"

"Yea!" I shouted. "Thanks, Trail Boss."

The Trail Boss ruffled up my hair, which was already ruffled badly, I was sure.

"Good landmarks, Arby," said Cowboy Brian. "We saw your arm band pieces on the trees as we came."

"Yeah," said the Trail Boss. "You owe me a dollar and twenty-five cents for that arm band." Then he laughed loud, so I knew he was kidding me about the dollar twenty-five.

"Let's sing as we walk back," said Cowboy Brian. "Stuart, what shall we sing?"

Stuart thought for a minute before he said, "The railroad song."

We were singing at the top of our lungs, "Dinah, won't you blow your horn," as they marched and I hobbled back into camp, leaning hard on Cowboy Brian. He said I'd live and that I could sleep in my wagon that night. Stuart was still shivering, though, and Cowboy Brian wanted to keep an eye on him, so he had to sleep at Doc's Hideaway that night.

"See you in the morning, Stuart," I said.

"See you, Tarzan," he said. "And thanks."

Cowboy Joe and Ray met me in Cowboy Brian's office. Cowboy Joe wanted to stay and talk to Stuart for a while.

"Help Arby hobble home," Cowboy Brian said to Ray.

"No problem," Ray said.

Ray walked me slowly back to my wagon. We sat on the steps and he told me his side of what had happened.

"Nobody knew that anything was wrong until after the ice-cream feed," said Ray.

"I can't believe I missed the ice-cream feed," I said.

"Never mind. It's just food," said Ray. "Now listen. The guys in Mustang Hollow were getting ready for bed, but you and Stuart weren't there. At first they thought maybe you were witnessing to him somewhere. Drew thought, though, that you would still be back before lights out."

"Which is true," I said.

"Cowboy Joe came in and asked whether any of them had overheard you saying anything that might be a clue to where you were, and they hadn't.

"Then Drew said if you were lost, they should ask me what to do. He figured that since you and I have been friends so long, I would know what you would do in an emergency situation. That Drew is a smart guy."

"He goes to Hope, can you believe it?" I said.

"Whoa," said Ray. He paused a minute to absorb this information. I could tell it was as difficult for him as it had been for me to find that a perfectly normal human being went to Hope. At last he collected himself and went on.

"I told them that if you were in any trouble whatever, especially if you were lost in the woods, that you would find a way to signal me. They said, 'Huh? What do you mean?' so I had to take precious minutes and explain about the signalman's corps."

"I had to do the same for Stuart," I said.

Ray went on to tell me how he had walked out to the clearing between the wagon train and the dining hall. Everyone else was looking around the camp, behind buildings and things, but he knew that I would find a high place to signal from.

"I told them to look up," he said. "And that's when we saw your S O S. Good thinking, that S O S."

"I was shouting, 'Look up!' at the same time that you were saying 'Look up!' It's funny."

"That's what happens when you've been friends forever. You think alike," said Ray.

I thanked Ray for helping me, and I told him what Stuart had said about his home and his dad and his interest in staying at camp to learn more about God.

"Good," said Ray. "I'll pray for him. He really needs the Lord."

I climbed up into the wagon, changed into my pajamas, and crawled into bed. As I stretched out my legs, I felt something slippery, soft, and cold.

"Aah! Oh! What in the world—" I shouted, pulling my legs out of my sleeping bag as quickly as I could.

I was greeted with muffled laughter and snickers all around.

"Welcome home, Arby," said Drew. "We thought we'd give you a coming home present." He laughed.

I turned on my flashlight and shone it into the sleeping bag. There was a plastic bag, the kind that have a sort of zipper at the top. It was filled with something multicolored and gooey.

I pulled it out. "What is it, guys?" I asked.

"It's your sundae," said Drew. "When I learned you were missing, I knew you'd need some cheering up when you were found, so I ran to the kitchen and found the cook still cleaning up after the ice-cream feed. I talked him into letting me have your sundae in a bag."

I laughed.

"Here," he said, handing me something. "It's a straw."

I took the straw, opened the bag a little and drank my sundae.

"Thanks, guys," I said. "You're the best."

20 A New Creature

I didn't get to see Stuart until after archery the next day. It was a beautiful morning; the birds were singing and flying around—hanging around camp like there was no better place in the world to be. Things look so much nicer in the day than at night. This is particularly true if you've spent a good part of the night sitting on a rock in the cold, wondering if anyone was looking for you.

I hit the target three times, tried to hop around in my happiness, and fell down on my backside.

After archery, there were a few minutes before wagon time, and I limped over to the infirmary to check on Stuart.

Cowboy Brian was sitting on a stool next to Stuart. He held an open Bible.

"C'mon in, Arby," he said. "I was just telling Stuart here about how God saves sinners."

I grinned and sat down at the end of Stuart's bed. "How are you doing?" I asked him.

"Pretty good," he said. "Boy, what a night we had, huh?"

"Yeah, but let's not do it again, okay?"

We three laughed: me sitting on the end of the bed, Stuart in bed, and Cowboy Brian, nurse extraordinaire, sitting on a stool, sharing the gospel with Stuart.

I listened while Cowboy Brian told Stuart about the sinfulness of all people.

"Like my dad, huh?" Stuart said.

"Yeah, and like me and you and Arby," Cowboy Brian said. "We're all sinners. All the time we want to go our own way, not God's way."

"Like when I went into the woods," said Stuart.

"Like when I complain about my brother," I said.

"Like when I drowned my cat in a well," said Cowboy Brian.

"You what—" Stuart and I said together.

Cowboy Brian smiled. "It was a long time ago."

"So you're all just as bad as me," Stuart said. "So then why are you going around here pretending to be such goody-goodies all the time and big-shot Christians and—" There was an edge to his voice and it worried me.

"Exactly my point, Baltz," said Cowboy Brian. "We *are* sinners. But Arby and I are Christians. That means we've recognized that we can't please God by ourselves. No matter what we do, we aren't able to get out from under our sins."

I nodded. I remembered that horrible feeling I'd had before I was saved, when I knew I was a sinner going to hell but there was nothing I could do about it.

Cowboy Brian continued. "But God loved us and sent His Son Jesus Christ to earth to die for us. His death paid the penalty for our sins. The Bible tells us that if we will acknowledge Christ as Lord of our lives and trust Him to save us, He will forgive us our sins."

"So," Stuart said slowly, "if I say I trust Jesus, then I'm saved. Okay, I'll say it: I trust Jesus."

I smiled. There it was. Stuart was saved.

"No, not exactly," said Cowboy Brian. I took a sharp breath. What did he mean *no, not exactly?*

"Becoming a Christian isn't just saying nice-sounding words and making a bigger effort to live a better life," said Cowboy Brian. "Becoming a Christian means turning away from your sinful life and turning to the Savior. It means following Christ—living like Him, living for Him, allowing Him to show Himself to others through you, trusting Him, believing Him. It's a total change of heart and mind."

I squirmed in my seat on the edge of the bed. What Cowboy Brian was saying bothered me.

"Cowboy Brian," I said, "shouldn't Stuart just pray to accept Christ so he won't go to hell? Then after that we could tell him about all this other stuff."

"Hell?" said Stuart. "What do you mean *hell?*"

"All this other stuff," said Cowboy Brian, "is the gospel, Arby. Salvation is not just putting a quarter in the God-machine and watching eternal life fall out into your hands. It's an all-out commitment to Christ."

"Hell?" said Stuart again. "What are you talking about? Is there really a hell? I thought Grandma Ellie just talked about hell to scare me into being good."

"Yes, Stuart. Hell is a real place," Cowboy Brian said, still looking at me. "Hell is the wages of sin. Stuart, what does your mom do?"

"Nothing so bad she should go to hell!"

"That's not what I meant. I meant, what does she do for a living?"

"Well, she's a waitress." Stuart swallowed.

"And what does she get for all her work?"

"She says she gets a lot of headaches and a little bit of money."

"Right," said Cowboy Brian. "The headaches and the money are the wages of being a waitress. That's what she gets paid. And the Bible tells us that the wages of sin—what we get paid for being sinners—is death. It means eternal death. Hell."

All this time Cowboy Brian was talking to Stuart, but he was looking at me. I was feeling more and more uncomfortable. I wanted to get out of there, but I didn't know why. After all, I was a Christian already. I'd been saved for a couple of years.

"So, since I'm a sinner, I go to hell." Stuart's voice was firm.

"Right. Unless you accept the grace of God and follow Jesus Christ as your Savior."

"Whoa," said Stuart. "I'd better think about this."

Whoa, I thought. I've got some things to think about too.

Cowboy Brian asked us to bow our heads, and he prayed that God would show Himself to Stuart and that we would all be followers of Christ.

After the amen, Stuart asked if he could go back to the wagon.

"It's up to you," Cowboy Brian said. "If you feel okay, you're okay."

"I'm okay," Stuart said, throwing off the covers. He was still wearing yesterday's clothes, and they were all wrinkly. Which meant he looked like just about everyone else in camp.

"Hey, Arby," Cowboy Brian's voice stopped me at the door. "Every so often I hear a message in church that makes me wonder if I ever really understood the gospel before."

I looked at the floor. So, he could tell. He could tell I'd thought all a person had to do was pray to accept Christ and

God would give him eternal life. That's all I had done when I was saved, just prayed, and got up off my knees saved.

"You just need to accept Christ to be saved, Arby. You've done that, right?"

"Yes, sir."

"I wanted Stuart to know it's not saying the words that saves a person. It's the grace of God through Christ. When you prayed to accept Christ, were you trusting your own words or were you trusting God?"

"God," I said quietly. "I didn't want to go to hell."

"Right," he said. Then he smiled and pushed me gently out into the sunny day. "We've got another week of camp to go, Arby. Why don't you come on over one day when you're not busy, and I'll show you some things in the Bible about following Christ. I think you'll find it interesting."

"Okay," I said. "I will."

I walked into the sunshine smiling. It was funny. I thought I'd come to camp just to kick a few pine cones, eat a few unhealthy meals, and hang around Ray. Instead, I'd seen almost nothing of Ray, made new friends, and gotten an invitation from Cowboy Brian to discuss the Bible man to man. And camp was only half over.

The Trail Boss spoke that night about abiding in Christ. We needed to be Christians, he said, in every part of our lives.

"On the ball field, you can be fair. In the classroom, you can be honest and not cheat. At home, you can be generous with your time and work."

That one got to me. I like to be selfish with my time, doing what I want to do when I want to do it. And I only do the chores I'm assigned. Maybe, to show my love for God and for my folks, I could help out more. There would be more work now that Grandma Parsons was coming to live with us.

"Some of you have Christian homes and go to Christian schools," the Trail Boss said. I perked up. That was me he was talking about now. "Be thankful for that. Do your best work. If you go to a Christian school, be a Christian there. If you go to a public school, be a Christian there. If you're homeschooled, be a Christian there. Wherever you are, whatever happens, trust the Lord to help you live for Him."

I looked up at the stars. I love the stars. There are millions of stars, billions or trillions maybe. God knew every one of them by name, like He knew every one of us. I was in His keeping, and everything—even sharing a room with Dell—was in His plan and care.

My thoughts were interrupted by the Trail Boss saying "Amen." I hadn't even known he was praying, I was so absorbed in my own thoughts. Maybe when I got a chance to talk to Cowboy Brian next week, he would help me learn to focus on what other people were saying for a change!

"Okay, guys," he said, "for our snack time tonight, we have a very special treat. It'll be explained by the counselor from Mustang Hollow, Cowboy Joe! Let's give him a round of applause."

We Mighty Mustangs rose to our feet to clap for our counselor—known to us privately as "Principal Joe, the Chocolate Man"—and we shouted our cheer as loudly as we could. Cowboy Joe ran down the steps.

He stood in front of the fire and smiled broadly. "Tonight's snack," he said, "is a melty sensation! See it drip! Feel it sliding down your throat!"

Boys started shouting things like "What? What is it?"

"It's peanut butter s'mores!" shouted Cowboy Joe.

"Yea!" shouted everyone. Everyone except me.

"Oh no," I groaned. "Not this again. I'll get sick."

"Arby," said Drew, "don't be silly. You got sick because you ate six of them. Just eat two and you'll be okay."

"Oh," I said. Just two.

We broke up into groups and went to several different fire circles. There was a box of supplies at each fire ring and enough skewers for all the kids.

Suddenly I had a question. "Hey, Cowboy Joe." I ran up to him and pulled on his sleeve, even though he was very busy telling people what to do.

"What, Arby?"

"Are there any Christian kids at your reform school?"

"Some. Why?"

"I want to know—can they, well, can they live for Christ even there?"

"You can live for Jesus anywhere, Arby. At any time. In any situation."

Anywhere, at any time, in any situation. I thought about a verse I had learned in Sunday school a long time ago: *I can do all things through Christ which strengtheneth me.*

"What is the big deal, Arby?" said Stuart later—as I was finishing my fifth peanut butter s'more and wishing I had stopped at three. "Why are you so worried about being a good Christian in a hard situation? You're a good kid, and besides, your situation isn't hard."

"Well, it's . . . it's," I couldn't tell him. His home problems were real problems and mine were nothing.

"What is it?" said Drew, who had come up behind Stuart. They stood there now, demanding to know what my problem was.

"I'm going to have to share a room with Dell," I said miserably.

There it was. Out in the open for them to ridicule. My puny little problem. I was upset because I was going to have to give up my private room, when other people, like Stuart, had tough things to deal with, like helping his mom out with the bills.

There was silence for a moment and then Stuart spoke.

"Well, Arb. You and I are practically neighbors, you know. So if you get sick of Dell, you can just come over and see how the other half of the world lives—get some perspective, you know." He slapped me on the back and laughed.

"Yeah," said Drew. "And then you can ride over to Hope School and—"

He was interrupted by Cowboy Joe shouting, "Last call for s'mores!"

"Come on, guys," I said, "let's get another one!"

Morse code

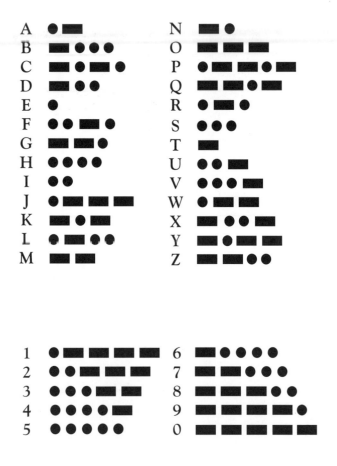

Start	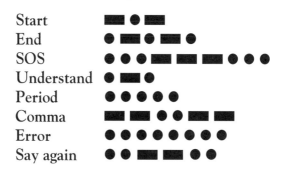
End	
SOS	
Understand	
Period	
Comma	
Error	
Say again	

●■■ ●●●● ●■ ■ ■●● ■■■

■●●● ●■● ■■■ ■●■ ● ■●

●■■●■ ●● ●■■●■ ● ●●● ■■●●■

■●■■ ● ●■●● ●■●● ■■■ ●■■

●■■●■ ●■ ●● ■● ■ ■■●●■

●■ ■● ■●● ■●● ●■● ●■ ■■● ■■■ ■● ●●●

●●●● ●■ ●●●■ ● ●● ■●

■●■● ■■■ ■■ ■■ ■■■ ■● ?

●●■● ●● ■● ■●● ■■■ ●●■ ■

●● ■● ■ ●●●● ● ■● ● ■●●■ ■

●■ ●■●● ■●●● ■●■■ ■●●● ■■■ ■■■ ■●■■

●●●●●